Second CHANCE at love

MIA LONDON

This is a work of fiction. Names, characters, places and incidents either are the product of the author's imagination or are used factitiously, and any resemblance to actual persons, living or dead, business establishments, event or locales is entirely coincidental.

Publisher: Mia London Books
PO Box 93852
Southlake, TX 76092

Edited by Traci Hall
Cover design by BookCover Kingdom

Acknowledgements

To my dear friend, you know who you are.
Thank you for everything.
Sometimes you give before I even ask.

Chapter One

RACHEL DRAGGED THE tines of her fork up the mound of potato, then squashed it flat. Without bothering to take a bite, she built up the ivory mountain and squished it again. Mashed potatoes had to be the most boring food ever. If Rachel had the energy, she would likely cry over her dinner plate.

Ethan was at his friend's house three doors down, working on a school project, but she knew her son was more likely to be playing video games than studying. Well, she told herself, how serious could the project be in the fourth grade?

Her daughter, Violet, scampered down the stairs and rushed to the laundry room to retrieve her jacket and shoes.

"Mom, Teagan's here," the eleven-year-old announced. Teagan Price was Violet's best friend for the past three years. She lived just a neighborhood over, and her mother would pick up Violet if she'd already planned to be in the car.

Rachel glanced at her daughter's plate which was mostly

clear. Violet definitely preferred chicken nuggets to chicken marsala.

"Okay, sweetie. If Mrs. Price can't drop you back off, I'll pick you up."

"Thanks," Violet called as she tugged her backpack over her shoulder and headed out the door.

Rachel sat at the secondhand round kitchen table she hated, wondering if this was what life as a divorcee would be like. Alone with the dishes from a meal she hated. She'd picked out the rectangular table for this kitchen, but it now resided at her ex's. What kind of jerk would take the family dining table just because he could?

Bastard.

At least she'd gotten the house, the wine collection, and the big screen TV.

The divorce had been official just a year, and admittedly, she was still adjusting.

Weekends meant cleaning the house from top to bottom, running the kids to *their* activities and errands, and then collapsing at night in front of the TV with Netflix, too tired to enjoy the peaceful view of the lake out back. During her weekends with the kids, they could watch a movie together and share a bowl of popcorn. On weekends Violet and Ethan were at their dad's, she'd do her own thing, like shop and visit with friends, but her life had become rather monotonous.

God, she was pitiful.

Rachel's two priorities in life at the moment were her kids and her job—both brought her so much joy. She was a rare breed of person who looked forward to Mondays. Work excited her. Her job as an administrative assistant to the president of Blazer Electronics, a mid-sized electronics company, was rewarding and sometimes challenging. Her boss treated her as an equal, demanded a lot from her, and paid her well for it.

She rose and gathered her and Violet's plates, scraping the potatoes into the trash. "Might not be a glamorous life but it is mine," she muttered to herself. And truly she'd rather be a little bored than married to Richie.

On Monday, Rachel arrived at eight o'clock instead of nine to work because she needed to leave early for Violet's try-out. Her daughter played the flute with the sixth-grade band. The school district had been invited to be part of a competition in Austin, and eight students from each grade were chosen to represent the district. Violet loved music and playing the flute, and practiced every chance she could— including the time she'd taken the flute into the bathroom as she waited on the hot water. Rachel was excited for her baby girl and wanted to be there to support her.

Rachel's boss, Roger Brennan, stepped into her oversized cubicle shortly before lunch. He'd already ditched his suit jacket and tie. He was barely six feet tall, had a large widow's peak in his light brown hair, and a smile that made everyone feel comfortable.

"Rachel, would you type this in an email? Send it to Larry and Suzanne in Procurement, and copy me on it—I need them on my calendar."

"Sure," she replied, taking the paper he handed her.

She read the note as he walked away. There appeared to be a concern about getting material from Sierra Leone in time for a client's deadline. Roger wanted an update *ASAP*.

Blazer had a source in Sierra Leone for necessary rare earth elements found in parts of Africa.

Roger was not your typical boss. He considered everyone in the company *family*. All employees were his friends, inside and outside of the office. But he could also be direct and firm when he meant business. Investors knew it, vendors knew it, and employees knew it.

After wrapping up her work for the day, Rachel slipped on her coat, turned off her monitor, and went to tell her boss she was leaving.

She strode into Roger's spacious office where he sat at his desk and snuck a quick peek at her watch. Six minutes before the traffic started to get crazy.

"Okay, Roger, I'm heading out. Just checking to see that you got the email before I take off." She hoped he'd say all was fine.

"Yes, thanks." He drew his attention away from his computer screen, looking as if he'd just seen something humorous. "I'm good. Tomorrow we can tackle the trip to

Palo Alto. I want Trey Wilkins to attend as well."

Blazer had a big prospect in Palo Alto. If the sales team wanted Roger there, that meant they stood a high chance of getting the deal. "Sounds good. I have calls rolling to voicemail."

"Perfect. Tell Violet I said good luck. Thanks again, Rachel."

She pivoted and barely made it over the threshold when she ran smack-dab into a wall of muscle.

Oomph!

A tall, dark-haired man smiled down at her. She stumbled back. His subtle hint of sandalwood cologne circled her, lifting her into a glorious brain fog. "Oh." Her hand went to her heart. "I'm terribly sorry." She stepped to the side.

"Rachel? Rachel Johnson?" His eyebrows lifted as he talked over her apology.

Her brow furrowed. This man knew her, but she didn't know him. After six years at Blazer, she knew most everyone in Roger's circle, from vendors to his wife and kids—she'd even met his housekeeper.

This delicious man, she did not know.

"Yes?"

"Oh, wow. Funny running into you. Here." He reached into his suit jacket pocket, retrieved a white envelope, and handed it to her.

What is this? Was she getting served? She bit her cheek and resisted the deep desire to run.

The envelope's paper was far too nice to be a court or government document.

"Cheryl can't make it to the ARC Gala. She told me to ask you instead."

"Cheryl?"

"Yes, Cheryl Moorland. So, here I am asking." His boyish grin on a mature face could make a woman swoon.

"Hunter!" Roger called from his office. "Get in here. You've got to see this."

The mystery man named Hunter smiled toward Roger and said, "Be right there." Turning back to her, his head tipped slightly as he asked, "Did she not call you?"

"No, but I don't know—"

"Well, I'm sure she will. I hope you're free Thursday night?" His lips pressed together. "It doesn't really start until eight."

What was going on and who was Cheryl Moorland? She lifted the envelope to return to him. "I think there is—"

"No, please don't say no." He stepped closer, his eyes pleading with her. "Cheryl will call you later and explain everything." His warm hands cupped hers, gripping the envelope tighter in her grasp.

"Hunter," Roger called again, an eager tone to his voice.

Hunter smiled directly at her. His gaze scanned her face, stopping for a fraction of a moment at her lips.

His looks were distracting. The words stalled in her throat. A thirty-nine-year-old mother of two energetic, almost-teenagers and assistant to a successful CEO of a growing electronics company was *rarely* at a loss for words. But now, nothing.

"I'll see you Thursday," Hunter said softly before releasing her hands and strolling into Roger's office. "You sure are getting impatient in your old age," she heard Hunter tell her boss.

Rachel stared down at the envelope. What was this about? She read the time on her phone. *Shit!* Two minutes later than she should have left. She would have to sort this out tomorrow, because right now her flute-player extraordinaire was expecting her number one fan to be sitting front row.

Rachel sat in the school auditorium with other parents, watching the sixth-graders audition. Immense pride bubbled inside her and was hard to contain. All Violet's extra practice had paid off. Afterward, there was a short break while the sixth-graders left with their parents and the seventh-graders set up for their turn.

She shuffled through the crowd of parents in the hall to meet their children. "Baby, you were amazing. You should be very proud of yourself."

"Thanks, Mom." Her daughter, with sandy-blonde hair like hers and precious pink lips, looked up with a glimmer of hope in her blue eyes.

"So when will you hear if you made it?"

"Mr. Hoth said in a week or two." Violet locked her flute case and stood. "Let me get my stuff and we can get out of here. I have a lot of homework to do."

"Okay." As Rachel waited on Violet, she shot a text to Bethany, the babysitter.

Wrapping it up at school. Should be home in 15.

Within a minute, Bethany replied.

Ethan wants to know if you can get pizza for dinner.

That sounded like a better option than what Rachel had planned. Dinner would have been like what she'd had growing up—a brown thing, a white thing, and a green thing. She typed.

Sure. See you soon.

Rachel dialed the local pizzeria and ordered an extra-large, loaded pizza. She could easily whip up a side salad with what was in her fridge at home.

She slipped her phone in her purse and the crisp white invitation she'd received earlier stared back at her. She bit her cheek. *Would it be bad to at least glance at the thing? The seal on the envelope will be broken*, she told herself.

"Okay, Mom, I'm ready." Her daughter beamed up at her eager to leave.

Rachel closed her purse. "Right. Need me to carry something?"

"No. I got it."

As they walked toward the parking lot, Rachel shared, "Your brother wants pizza, so we need to stop at Aldo's on the way home."

"Yay." Violet bounced on her tiptoes. "They have the *best* pizza."

She smiled at her daughter. If her kids were happy, she'd consider this a great day.

~

What a fortunate turn of events, Hunter Baron thought as he left Roger's office and got into the elevator to the lobby.

He owned a consulting firm that specialized in helping companies in extreme flux, and Hunter depended on referrals to keep the sales pipeline full. The ARC Gala was a major opportunity for networking and making pivotal connections in the business world.

Usually, Cheryl Moorland attended these events with Hunter, with Ken's blessing—her husband, and his best friend. As the head of the largest hospital chain in the southwest, Cheryl knew a slew of people and could make introductions that Hunter wouldn't otherwise find.

When Cheryl had called him that morning and complained she felt the flu coming on, his heart sank. But then she'd quickly followed up with a plan to salvage his night. She happened to be close friends with a PR executive, Rachel Johnson, who was also a highly connected member of the community. Cheryl assured him that she'd ask Rachel to step in for the evening.

"Phew," he'd semi-joked over the phone. The prior year, he'd garnered three excellent contacts from the gala.

Cheryl had added that Rachel worked in the Palladium Building on the thirty-eighth floor for Watson, Bradley, and Chalmers," her sluggish voice came through the phone.

Serendipitous for him to drop in on Roger Brennan, owner of Blazer Electronics, who had offices in that same building. They'd been college roommates and remained good friends.

Cheryl had remarked dryly that he needed to find a date besides her for these events. It was time. He stepped out of the building to the sidewalk, the conversation playing over in his head.

Hunter didn't agree. Cheryl was perfect in the role of business escort. Fun, knowledgeable, and she understood his past. He supposed he could hit the golf course to form connections, but he'd rather toast wine than drive a cart. Golf took too much time. Life was short as both Cheryl and Ken were aware.

Hunter had lost his wife eight years ago, just as his company was taking off. He'd dived into his business after mourning hard. He'd decided then and there serious dating was out of the question. He simply wouldn't tarnish the memory of his wife and their life together by getting into another long-term relationship.

He and Jessica had had a future planned. After focusing

on their careers, they would start a family. Every year, they'd make a list of what they wanted to accomplish—for the house, or trips they wanted to take, or anything. It had been so freakin' effortless being married to Jessica.

Then in the blink of an eye, their dreams, and Jessica, had disappeared.

Some days, the pain of missing her was so crippling, Hunter didn't want to do a damn thing. It could still hit him sometimes, after eight years.

Hunter exhaled as he got into his car for the drive home. He wouldn't focus on that. He couldn't.

The good news was he now had an escort for the gala, and things were lookin' up.

Rachel—wearing a lovely smile and the sweet scent of vanilla—was like a breath of fresh air. It was as if he'd manifested her the moment he'd walked into the building. He didn't even need to make the trip to the thirty-eighth floor.

He was still chuckling once he reached his place, and switched on his over-sized monitor in the home office. There was always work to do.

Yup, this was gonna be a great week.

Chapter Two

BRIGHT AND EARLY the next day, Roger was already in his office by the time Rachel arrived. He dashed around like he was late for something, shuffling papers on his desk and muttering to himself. His coat and a folded tie were draped over his luggage by the wall.

Something's up.

She stepped into his office as the door was wide open. "Hey, Roger. What's goin' on?"

"Rachel, I'm glad you're here. I need to go to Sierra Leone. Something's come up and if I don't straighten it out, we'll miss the commitment date for CCE. Would you get me a ride to the airport? I'll leave my car here."

"Sure." CCE was a major new account, one the company, Roger especially, had fought hard to get.

She spun around, hung up her coat, and dialed the car service from her desk. As her computer came alive, she returned to Roger's office. "What else do you need?"

Roger tugged at his hair as he scanned his desk. "I think I have everything." He slipped on his jacket and pocketed his tie.

"Do you have your passport?"

He patted his chest pocket. "Yup."

"Okay, what else can I do for you from here?"

Her boss switched off his monitor and locked his desk drawers, a ritual he performed when he left for the day. "I'll let you know, but don't forget that cell service can be spotty. I'll try to email as well. It should be no more than three days. I'll keep you posted, but right now all I need is for you to cancel my appointments." He crossed the carpeted floor and flipped the light switch. "Wish me luck."

"Good luck," she called after him as he strode down the hall, the elevator arriving quickly to the sixteenth floor of a fifty-six-story building.

Rachel stashed her purse in a bottom drawer and hooked a lock of hair behind her ear. What a whirlwind.

She inhaled a clarifying breath and got to work changing Roger's appointments for the next three days. Sudden trips like this rarely happened; it must be serious for him to take a twenty-hour flight. She only hoped Roger got everything squared away. The relationship with the company's Sierra Leone supplier was crucial.

The morning flew by in a flurry. Rachel had been slammed with Roger's unexpected trip. Calls, emails, people dropping by—so much to do, and everything urgent. The list of things to share and clarify with Roger grew by the minute. She couldn't take the time to leave, so she ordered lunch from the first-floor deli.

She pulled out cash for the delivery boy who set her turkey club with a side salad on her desk and left. As she stuck her wallet back in her purse, Hunter's invitation caught her eye.

Crap! I've got to get this thing returned.

She'd completely forgotten to ask Roger who the heck this handsome Hunter was... Rachel pulled out the envelope and examined it. What was the invitation for anyway? And who was this other Rachel Johnson?

Within a month of changing her driver's license and social security information to her married name, the wrong mail and phone calls had started. She'd had no idea she had just "created" a popular name by marrying Richie. The barrage had slowly dissipated.

After thirteen years of marriage, she and Richie were now officially divorced. Rachel had considered changing back to her maiden name but the confusion of mistaken identity had died down. Not to mention, she thought keeping her last name the same as the kids would be best.

Rachel stared at the beautiful, crisp stationary, the kind wedding invitations were printed on. She *had* to know what it was for. Hunter had mentioned a gala and a woman who was supposed to call her. He hadn't called, and neither had the woman. So, she gently slipped the flap loose on the envelope and pulled out the card nestled inside.

Please join Animal Rescue and Care
for the
15th Annual Black Tie Gala

Thursday, January 18th
7:00 PM – 12:00 Midnight

Dinner | Entertainment | Silent Auction

PROCEEDS FROM THIS EVENT BENEFIT
THE ANIMAL RESCUE AND CARE (ARC) NON-
PROFIT.

Wow! This was certainly *not* something meant for her. Maybe *a* Rachel Johnson, but not her. The kind of invites she received were almost always for the kids. She'd occasionally get a wedding invite, but nothing like this.

Wasn't that a pretty invitation? She ran a finger over the embossed lettering.

She shook her head. She had to give this back to Hunter, and the sooner the better. Now, to find him.

Rachel glanced at the time on her monitor. Her boss wouldn't have landed yet, not for a twenty-hour flight. She'd need to wait hours before she could call him during his layover.

Work was the priority. She took the last bite of her salad and focused on the ten new emails that loaded her inbox.

By the end of the day, Rachel was both exhilarated and exhausted. She'd never felt so needed, so necessary. The clock read five-fifteen. Roger would likely be at his layover city.

She dialed and listened to his cell phone ring. *Oh, that's a good sign.* It rang several more times then rolled to voicemail. Asking about Hunter was not a message she wanted to leave.

Dammit!

"Hey, Roger, just checking in, making sure you arrived safely. Call when you can."

Rachel nibbled on her lower lip. She did the math in her head. With the long flight and six-hour time difference, she could maybe reach him between meetings.

"I'll try again first thing in the morning," she whispered to herself. The following day was Wednesday; she had no choice.

She shut down her computer, locked her drawers and Roger's office. After the busy day, she couldn't wait to get home, and hear from her kids about their day at school.

This was real life to her—her kids, friends, and family—not some bougie-bougie gala.

After dinner, Ethan finished his math worksheet, and Rachel allowed him some video game time before he had to shower. Violet worked at the kitchen table while Rachel cleaned up and washed a load of towels.

"Mom, I think I'm done. I need to ask Mrs. Stewart about one thing, but that's it," Violet announced.

"Okay Want me to check it?"

"Nope. I'm gonna take a shower now."

"All right, sweetie." Rachel pecked the top of her daughter's head as Vi strode by on the way upstairs.

She had good kids; Violet was the most responsible. Ethan was the cuddly one, and at nine, she hoped she had a few more years to enjoy that.

Rachel flipped off the kitchen lights and sank into her comfy couch in the family room to call her best friend, Alexis.

"Hey, chica! How was your day?" Alexis answered.

"Busy. Roger had an unexpected trip to Sierra Leone, so I was slammed." Rachel sipped her chardonnay as she stretched her legs out across the sofa.

"Wow. Sierra Leone. Sounds fun."

Rachel had seen the pictures and heard the stories from Roger. The place was beautiful—mountains on one side, ocean on the other. Lush green gardens and friendly inhabitants made Rachel want to go sometime too. "We should go."

"But wait, before we go any further, we need to talk about your birthday."

Her birthday. Rachel let out a sigh. She would turn forty and wasn't thrilled with the idea. She wasn't thrilled about growing old, period.

"Okay, what's the plan?" She was resigned to letting Lexi throw her a party even though she'd rather it just be the two of them. It wasn't like she had a date or someone she was interested in—but that was a different subject.

"First off, Richie has the kids, right?"

"Yes." Lexi knew the answer to that.

"Great. Next you have two choices for dinner—Brio or Rafele's."

"Oh, I love them both."

"I know you do," Lexi replied matter-of-factly. "I'll see who can take reservations for a large party at seven-thirty."

"Okay. What are we doing afterward?"

"*That's* a surprise. Next, the guest list. I'll email you who I've got on the evite list. Add or subtract as you wish."

A surprise? That had Rachel a little worried. Lexi's surprises were almost always over the top. "I don't need a lot of people there."

Alexis scoffed. "I know, but you should celebrate. This is a big birthday, sister. We're doing it in style."

She groaned, and Alexis laughed.

"So, tell me what else is going on?"

The invitation to the Gala sat in her purse like a beacon. "Well, funny you should ask. A man came to see Roger yesterday—he thought I was someone else and handed me an invitation to some Gala Thursday night."

"Wait! What? The ARC Gala?"

"Um, I think so. Something about animals."

"Yeah, that's it. You were invited to the Gala?" Lexi's voice rose an octave. "That's all I've been hearing about the past week from the girls and my clients." When Alexis talked about *the girls*, she referred to her outstanding team of employees at her company.

Alexis King was a shoe designer who'd also created her own self-labeled company, AK Designs, although she did a lot less "designing" lately. The company had only four stores, but most of its business came from sales through department stores and online. Alexis was incredibly successful. Rachel had no doubt she'd been outfitting women who planned to attend this extravagant event.

"Well, I'm sure it's a mistake. He wanted another Rachel Johnson which is such a shame—he was very handsome."

"Handsome? How handsome?"

She sighed and brought up his image. "He was tall, had brown hair with a little gray, sorta brown-gray eyes. And a breathtaking smile."

"Ooh, sounds yummy! Plus, that event is like two-hundred and fifty dollars a person. So you gave him back the invitation?"

"Well, no. I had to rush out, and he went into Roger's office." She pulled a pillow out from behind her so she could recline more on the sofa. "I don't even know anything about him except his first name is Hunter."

"Ha! Well, Rach, just go." Lexi's smile spiraled through

the phone.

Rachel's eyebrows rose. "I can't 'just go.' He's expecting someone else. It might be a blind date or something since he didn't recognize my face, but it's not meant for me. I'm calling Roger in the morning so I can track him down and return it."

"That's too bad. I bet you'd have fun."

Rachel just laughed. She didn't do these kinds of affairs and soirées. Hell, she barely knew how to spell the word *soirée*. No, the sooner she got that invitation back to Hunter, the sooner she would be at peace with the whole matter.

"Look, I gotta go, babe. Ethan hasn't been in the shower yet and it's almost eight-thirty."

"Okay, hugs to the kids. I'll send over the list. Talk to you later." The line went dead.

She slipped her cell phone into her purse and brushed a finger over the brilliant white envelope. She allowed herself a moment to fantasize about the Gala—dancing in some long, flowing gown with Hunter's arms wrapped around her. He would smile at her just as he had Monday, like she was the only person in his world.

Her tummy did a little flip. Nice dream, but not realistic. She was a middle-aged divorced woman with two children. The highlights in her life revolved around her kids and their successes. If they were happy, then she was too.

"Mom!" Ethan called down to her from the upstairs hall.

"Yes?" She walked to the kitchen and stacked her wine glass in the dishwasher.

"Can I have Tim over this weekend to play video games?"

That sounded a bit suspicious. "Sure. Is there something more to that?"

"He's grounded and can't play for a week."

Ah. Now I know the rest of the story. She had to chuckle. Ethan was always honest. He may get in trouble from time to time, especially in the months after their father had moved out and divorce proceedings started, but Rachel could always count on Ethan's honesty. "Okay. Now, please get in the shower."

After the kids were tucked into their beds, Rachel flipped off the lights and made her way to her bedroom on the first floor. The furnishings and décor were all original from when she and Richie had moved in. It had a more masculine feel that Rachel found boring—dark colors, geometric patterns, uninspiring furniture. Her life was already boring enough. Maybe she should budget for an update. She could comb those online buy/sell sites and possibly find a great deal on some furniture, one-of-a-kind pieces. She nodded as she stripped out of her clothes and washed her face.

How pretty would that look? A new king-sized bed in a rich wood tone, champagne-colored bedspread and linens, luxurious pillows, and possibly long silk drapes to match. And a chaise. She'd always wanted a chaise lounge in her bedroom, positioned in the corner. "There's room," she said to no one.

She slipped on a long cotton nightshirt and turned off the bedside lamp, too tired to pick up her ereader. An image of Hunter flashed in her mind. She smiled and drifted off into a sound sleep, hoping the next day she could track down this anonymous man.

Chapter Three

ENERGY PULSED THROUGH her Wednesday morning as Rachel prepared to tackle the day. She had a list a mile long for Roger, *including* finding out about the mysterious Hunter. She had to return that stinking invitation right away. Guilt had begun to eat at her because she hadn't yet.

The intended "Rachel" might be mad once she learned Rachel had *her* invitation to the Gala. And not just because it looked like it would be an amazing event, but also because Hunter was handsome as hell, and any woman would give their last hundred bucks for a date with him. That smattering of gray hair at his temples and sideburns had Rachel wondering how old he was. Maybe mid-forties. He had the most expressive brown-gray eyes, and a full head of thick hair that made Rachel want to take her time running her fingers through it.

She dropped the kids off at school, then entered her

office and started her morning routine—booting up the computer, hanging up her coat, stashing her purse, and putting on a pot of coffee.

She pulled her notepad with her list for Roger in front of her, then dialed his number. It would be two in the afternoon there. Immediately, the call rolled to voicemail.

Dang it!

She opened email, and thankfully, Roger had contacted her. A few random things she needed to do for him—letters, calls, and appointments. He'd apologized for not being able to call and complained about the horrible cell service.

She replied, confirming his requests, then listed what she needed from him. She ended with saying that she'd like to get in touch with Hunter, if Roger had his number?

Gees! Roger's probably gonna think I want to ask him out on a date or something. And what if he's married? That can't look good to my boss about his friend.

She had no choice so she sent the email, hoping for a fast reply.

As the hours passed, Rachel must have scanned her inbox a million times. "C'mon, Roger," she whispered out loud.

Finally, an hour before she wanted to head home, she received an email from her boss.

Praise the Lord!

She scanned the text—details and questions to her inquiries. Roger seemed to be under stress, as he'd made quite a few typos and errors in his reply, which wasn't like him. If they didn't get things ironed out, what would that mean for the company? For her job?

Oh gees!

She got to the end where he mentioned Hunter. *Great!*

No phone number. *What?*

All he wrote was, "Isn't he great?"

What!

Rachel wanted to scream. She'd waited all day, and that was all she got for her patience?

What the hell was she gonna do?

With her elbows resting on the arms of her chair, she tapped her fingernails rapidly against each other and stared at the screen. *Dammit!*

She could search the vendor/supplier database for his name. Roger had acted as if they were friends but he did that with everyone. A few keystrokes later, she had the contents open—no "Hunter" appeared anywhere in the database. On a whim, she hunted for "Cheryl Moorland." Nothing.

What could she do?

She reached for her purse and yanked out her cell phone.

"Hey, chica. What's up?" Alexis greeted her.

"Lexi, I need some advice."

"Okay. Are you all right? You sound stressed."

"I can't find out how to get a hold of Hunter."

"The hottie with the Gala invitation?"

"Yes. Roger's tied up in Sierra Leone. He hasn't given me Hunter's number."

"And you feel guilty about the invite?"

Rachel exhaled. "Yes." She tried not to whine.

"Babe, you're such a good person. Thank God, you're good enough for both of us..."

Rachel smirked. It was true. Wasn't it just last month Lexi tried to get her a massage at a very hush-hush place just outside of town? Rachel had the distinct impression Lexi knew all about this particular massage place and had probably gone a time or two. To *relax*.

"I have your solution," Lexi finally said.

"Great. What is it?" Rachel sat taller in her office chair.

"Go."

Did she hear that right? This was the *last* thing Rachel could do. "What?"

"Go to the Gala. And before you say no, hear me out." Her friend was brilliant, a little eccentric, and certainly a risk-taker, but smart as hell. "You have three choices. A, find Hunter or the *right* Rachel Johnson. Which isn't looking promising right now. B, don't go and see if there's any fall-out." Oh, that thought twisted a knot in her stomach. "Or C, you go. If he needs a date for this major event, at least he has you..."

A message dinged in Rachel's ear.

"In this dress."

Rachel opened the text to see a picture of a navy, floor-length, strapless ball gown hanging on a cloth-covered hanger. It was very simply gorgeous.

"Oh, Lex. That's beautiful."

"I bought it some years ago for the grand opening of Birmingham's, and never wore it. And I have a few ideas of the perfect heels to go with it."

Rachel stared at the dress wordlessly. She would love to wear that splendid gown, layers of chiffon cascading over her legs, chasing her as she spun around the dance floor in Hunter's arms. Nevertheless, this invitation wasn't meant for her. "I don't know, Lex."

"I do. You should go. This is a big deal, and if he arrives dateless, he'll be kicking himself for the whole 'mistaken identity' thing. You can save him."

She inhaled, mushing her lips together. Could she pull this off? Could she show up at this exclusive event, wearing an expensive ensemble, and at least temporarily serve as a date for someone who was likely very familiar with this kind of thing? This was a different world from where she lived, in many respects.

"The long silence tells me you're thinking about this. Well, stop thinking. I'll meet you at my house in thirty minutes." And her phone screen went blank.

Damn! She knows me too well.

Maybe Rachel should at least go try on the dress and shoes and perhaps with a stroke of luck, Roger would call her and it would all be a dream. *Isn't it the dead of night there?*

Or possibly Hunter would call her—he knew where she worked, after all.

Gees, what was she doing? This was crazy with a capital K.

Thirty minutes later, Rachel was in her best friend's bedroom, stripping out of her work clothes and laying them across Lexi's bed. The knot in her stomach grew to a small boulder. She hated not being able to locate Hunter and tell him the truth as much as she disliked going to such a formal event completely unprepared. The last formal event she'd attended was her wedding, and everyone knew how that ended.

"Here. Try this." Lexi held the strapless dress for Rachel to step into.

Lexi zipped up the back, and Rachel stared at her reflection. A gown of rich navy blue flowed and puddled to the floor. Her eyes went to her chest as the fabric pushed against her boobs. This dress was definitely made for a more svelte figure, more model-like, so Rachel and her C-cup boobs were just...

"Wow! That's much nicer on you than me."

Rachel wrinkled her nose. "I don't know, Lex. I'm sorta over-flowing here."

"Nonsense. That fits great. And it's okay to have the girls on display every once in a while."

"I look slutty." She pulled against the bodice.

"No, you don't. Slutty is when you're spilling out. That dress *accentuates*. You're gorgeous. Now, for the shoes." Lexi reached into the two large shopping bags she'd brought home from her store. All her designs, of course, and in Rachel's size.

Rachel sat on the bench at the end of the bed, ogling the beautiful creations as Lexi flipped off the lids. Navy, silver, and a combination of both. She slipped on a strappy pair of silver heels and rose. "Nice, but maybe too high," she said as she wobbled on the carpet back to the bench.

"Try these."

Rachel slid on a pair of suede peep-toe heels in navy. She stood and instantly fell in love. "Oh, Lex. These are beautiful." She went to the full-length mirror, turning this way and that, getting a good perspective of the entire ensemble. Words couldn't describe how incredible she felt. Elegant and sophisticated.

"Are those it?"

Rachel smiled at Lexi's reflection behind hers. "They are." The shoes were surprisingly comfortable. "You're really a great designer, Lex."

"I know." Lexi grinned, her blue eyes sparkling even more off the reflection of her pale aqua sweater. "Now, I have Milo coming over tomorrow to do your hair. Bring your makeup bag and undergarments. I'll have some jewelry laid out for us to go through."

Milo was another close friend of Lexi's who happened to be extraordinary with hair. He could book out three months in advance.

Alexis had thought of everything. Well, everything except a babysitter *and* telling her kids. She needed to get home and ask Bethany if she was free. If not, Rachel'd have to think of something else, because her parents and siblings had all moved out of Houston years ago. And she knew there was no way Alexis would let her off the hook now.

Over dinner, Rachel cautiously broached the subject of homework for the following night. She knew the kids would think their mother dating odd. Any previous dates she'd relegated to her off-weekends: the weekends Richie had the kids, so they'd been none the wiser.

This little announcement would certainly come as a surprise.

She cleared her throat. "Kids, tomorrow night I'm going out. Bethany will be here to babysit."

"Wait. It's Thursday," Violet said. "A school night."

"I know." Rachel expelled a slow breath. "You just told me that you have your projects under control."

"Do you have a *date*?" Ethan had two close friends whose parents were divorced, plus his own father was dating someone nine years younger than him.

"Kind of. Yes, it's an event."

They both looked at her and blinked.

"I met him through work, so it's sorta like a work date." Rachel hated the panic on their expressions.

That seemed to go down easier—both their little faces

relaxed in understanding. "Okay, Mom. Have fun." Violet dug into her beef stroganoff.

"Can we have tacos with Bethany?"

Rachel grinned. Ethan loved his junk food. All kinds of food really. He was due for another growth spurt.

Thursday was a day like no other. Her head was a jumbled mess, matching her insides. First, Rachel forgot to call back a department head with Roger's revised schedule. Then she sent two—count 'em *two*—emails to the wrong people. And she hardly touched her lunch. She didn't know if she'd make it through the day. On a positive note, the very brief email she'd received in the middle of the night from Roger was encouraging regarding their Sierra Leone supplier.

Now, Rachel sat at Alexis's kitchen table while Milo brushed through her shoulder-length hair. Thank God the blonde hid the gray that had started cropping up.

"What can we do with this hair?" Lexi asked, glancing from her to Milo.

Milo was eccentric in his tastes, wearing a pink shirt, camo pants, layered with a bright scarf and fitted jacket. And he made no apologies for it. He knew when it came to styling and coloring hair, he was one of the best.

He cocked his hip to the side and held his finger under his chin. "I'm feeling a little Renee Russo in The Thomas Crown Affair."

"You can do that?" Rachel lifted her eyebrows, loving that look.

"Darlin', I can do anything." Milo opened his Glitz Kit, crammed to the brim with flat irons, brushes, sprays, volumizers, pins, embellishments, and anything else a girl might need for beauty on the run.

Milo continued in a dry tone, "So ladies, I hate to bring up the obvious, but have y'all wondered if this is supposed to be a blind date? Set up by this Cheryl woman?"

"I did," Lexi announced as she filed her nails.

"What?" Rachel nearly gasped. "I could be going on someone else's blind date?"

She glanced at Lexi then Milo as they each smiled.

"I thought I was just saving him from having egg on his face since it seems like an important event, but..."

Lexi shook her finger. "Uh-uh. That's why I didn't mention it. You'll start worrying, so stop. You're going, whatever the reason, the decision has been made."

Rachel exhaled and bit her tongue as Milo worked his magic. She fought down her uneasiness and simply enjoyed her pampering session.

When Milo was done, neither of them uttered a word as they studied Rachel, then Milo said, "Next," and Lexi began painting her face. They wouldn't let her see any of the progress along the way, and it was killing Rachel. But admittedly, she *loved* being pampered. She rarely took the time for this kind of thing anymore. Despite the nerves, she felt like royalty. What girl wouldn't?

After the last swipe of the brush cross her lips, Alexis sat back and declared with a smile, "Dress time."

As they'd done the night before, Alexis helped her step into her gown, then her shoes. They perused the jewelry Lexi had laid out on her dresser.

Lexi lifted a dazzling, vintage-looking silver necklace with matching drop earrings. "Here. This is what you should wear."

Rachel slipped on the jewelry, and Alexis called for Milo.

He walked into the bedroom and gasped, his hand flying over his mouth.

Alexis turned her toward the full-length mirror so she could finally see what she looked like. She nearly gasped herself.

Before her stood a woman in a glamourous dress and shoes, with sparkling jewelry, perfect makeup, and the most beautiful updo she'd ever seen. She hardly recognized herself. She felt elegant and beautiful. It was surreal.

"Oh, I almost forgot." Lexi ran into the closet and came back with a matching navy clutch purse and wrap. "You may be a little cold, but you look fantastic, so that's all that counts."

They all chuckled.

Rachel's attention turned to the items in Lexi's hands and reality began to set back in. She tried desperately not to nibble off her lipstick.

Both Alexis and Milo beamed at her. "What do you think?" Milo asked.

"Fabulous. All eyes will be on you." Alexis nodded, scanning her up and down.

"That's what I'm afraid of," Rachel said, deciding that maybe she should stay home. She tried to hand back the clutch and wrap.

"Uh-uh." Milo stepped closer, resting his hands on her shoulders. "You can't back down now. You've come too far. And if it's a bust, hop in your car and high-tail it out of there."

He had a point. She could leave at any time.

"You can do this, Rach," Alexis assured her.

"I can do this," she repeated. She might appear amazing on the outside, but on the inside, she was a tangle of nerves.

"That's right." Milo nodded.

Rachel spun around to face her glam squad. "Thank you both so much. I couldn't have done it without you."

They smiled and hugged her, careful of the hair and makeup.

She couldn't put it off. Now was the moment of truth, in more ways than one.

Chapter Four

HUNTER WAS LATE. He *hated* being late. The meeting with Branson, Inc. had gone long so it had been unavoidable.

The five-man band played a classic piece from the fifties in the spacious ballroom, probably able to hold five-hundred people. The chandeliers sparkled along with the candles set at every black-clothed table. Hunter had been to a million of these kinds of functions. It was par for the course when running his own business that depended heavily on networking and relationship-building—which was why Cheryl's recommendation was crucial.

When Cheryl had called to say she couldn't make it, he'd been tempted to bail. He didn't give a rat's ass about the two-hundred and fifty dollar per plate ticket. That was a business expense Hunter budgeted for every year. Socializing and networking produced much more fruit than advertising ever would, so not having his best friend's wife on his arm to steer him through the maze of Houston's business elite was daunting.

Cheryl's proxy, Rachel Johnson, worked on the thirty-eighth floor, and his pal was on the sixteenth, so he'd stopped in to say hi. How serendipitous that he'd found Rachel coming out of Roger's office, where she'd nearly taken his breath away when she'd slammed square into his chest. He'd gotten lost in her sparkling indigo eyes and held her until she'd regained her footing but then didn't want to let go. He would have to remember to ask her how she knew Roger.

Cheryl had sent him a text yesterday to ask if he'd connected with Rachel and he'd told her yes.

Now, he stood off to the side entrance in the hotel's ballroom, searching for her.

What if she didn't show?

He had been rather uncongenial when he'd practically thrust the invitation into her hands. One look at her and he couldn't accept "no."

This was business, not a date. Still, when he'd given her the invite, he hadn't seen a wedding ring on her finger.

Hunter took a champagne flute from the waiter slowly making rounds through the crush.

He caught a glimpse of a blonde woman with her hair pinned up, wearing a long, flowing, strapless blue dress. He prayed that it was Rachel. She was gorgeous. He was captivated by her, and not the only one. He noticed several males discreetly tracking her. She seemed tentative, her gaze combing the room.

It *was* Rachel, perhaps looking for him. He wondered why she wasn't engaged in a conversation.

Before someone got the wrong idea that she was free, Hunter moved through the throng toward his elegant date, leaving his glass on an empty table.

"Good evening, Ms. Johnson," he said from behind her slender back.

She spun around in her heels—making her taller than at Monday's encounter—and smiled. His eyes instantly fixated on her lush lips, the peaks of her cupid's bow tempting him.

"Good evening. Please call me Rachel." She offered her hand.

He clasped it, enjoying the softness of her skin.

A waiter offered a full tray of sparkling flutes. "Rachel, you don't have a drink. Care to join me in a glass of champagne?" When she nodded, he retrieved two and handed her one. Their fingers brushed.

"Thank you."

She was enchanting. Graceful. And for a moment, he forgot he was there for business purposes. "You look incredibly lovely tonight."

Color rose in her cheeks as she glanced down at the champagne glass. Such an uncharacteristic move for a woman so well-connected.

"Thank you," she murmured, then lifted her head. "You're very handsome yourself."

"I want to apologize for being late."

"It's quite all right." Her eyes showed sincerity, and as he held her gaze, she blushed again and peered into her flute. Charming.

In an effort to keep their evening professional, he steered the conversation to business. "Did I miss anything?"

Her eyes shifted left and right, like she was searching for the answer.

"Um, dinner. They announced dinner." She nodded, pointing her chin to the far side of the ballroom where a line of tables were arranged, buffet-style.

That wasn't exactly the response he'd been expecting. He scanned the room, taking note of new and familiar faces. "Excellent. Have you eaten?"

"Not yet, but Hunter—"

That was the first time he'd heard his name cross her perfect lips. His stomach flipped.

"—I think I need to clarify something."

The band finished their instrumental number, and an older gentleman with salt-and-pepper hair, dressed in a tuxedo, took the stage. The crowd started to applaud, and Hunter leaned closer to Rachel's ear. "Wow. Is that Milton Hammerschmein? He's lost weight."

She lifted her gaze to meet his. "Uh, I have no idea."

He squelched a frown and turned his attention toward the stage. *She doesn't know?*

"Good evening folks, and welcome." The applause died down. "My name is Milton Hammerschmein, President of the

Board of Directors for ARC, Animal Rescue and Care. It's been several years since I've attended the gala, and I'm happy to report my improved health has allowed me to be here with you tonight." More applause. "Thank you. This is the fifteenth year of the ARC Gala. It is our biggest fundraiser, and it's so successful because of all of you and our most-generous sponsors. You have my gratitude." He bowed slightly at the additional applause. "The incomparable Catherine Shawl will be up later to talk to you more about the silent auction, but for now, I get to announce, the dance floor is open. Enjoy your evening." Milton handed the mic to a female singer who strode to his side.

The band began to play something Hunter recognized as a Tina Turner number.

Pivoting back to the lovely Rachel, he held out a hand. "Let's go get some dinner before it's all gone, shall we?"

She bit her lower lip briefly before nodding and placing her hand in his.

Hunter had to admit the evening wasn't playing out quite as he had envisioned. His tardiness was to blame. By this time, Cheryl would have introduced him to half a dozen successful business owners, helping to line his pockets with business cards he could call on later.

He mentally shook his head. His fault, not to mention that Rachel was no Cheryl. Rachel seemed unusually shy and she certainly hadn't taken the lead.

"This looks delicious," she said, taking two china plates

from the stack and handing one to him.

"It does." They proceeded down the leisurely moving line, filling their plates with shrimp scampi, tenderloin, garlic-sautéed green beans, rice pilaf, poached salmon, and numerous side dishes. "Have you been to the ARC Gala before?"

She glanced his way before ducking her head and putting a caprese salad on her plate. "No, and actually that's—"

"Hunter!" a familiar voice said. "You made it."

Hunter shifted around, balancing his plate. "Griffin. How's it going?" He shook hands with his old friend.

"Great! And who is your companion?"

"Rachel Johnson. Rachel, this is Griffin Washburn. We used to work together at E&Y."

They exchanged smiles since Rachel had her hands full. "Nice to meet you," she said in a gracious tone.

"Likewise." Griffin looked at him. "Let's get together soon for some squash. I'm eager to regain my championship title."

Hunter grinned. "You wish, but I'm more than willing to take your money again."

"Ha!" Griffin slapped him on the back. "I'll call you next week. Rachel. Have a good night, y'all."

Griffin walked off, and Hunter realized they had slowed the food line. They quickly served themselves a few more selections, and he scouted the seating area of the ballroom for an available table. "Over there." He gestured with a tilt of his head. He decided not to search out anyone he knew because he wanted to come up with a game plan for conquering the room.

They sat at a large round table for ten, in front of the picture windows facing the gardens. It was too dark to see anything but a few scattered low-lights along an empty path. Three people were across from them, engrossed in conversation. He expected more folks would join them shortly as people went through the buffet line.

Just as he spread the napkin over his lap, his clients Mitch and Lisa approached. "Hey, Hunter," Mitch said.

"Hey, you two." Hunter rose to shake hands and give Lisa a peck on the cheek. "I didn't know if you would make it."

"Wouldn't miss it," Mitch smirked as his eyes flashed to the left, hinting that it was more Lisa's idea of fun than his.

"And who is your precious date?" Lisa asked with a unusually bright smile.

"My apologies." His hand rested on Rachel's shoulder. "Rachel, please meet my best client and his wife, Mitch and Lisa Shaffer."

Mitch snorted. "I don't know about that." He leaned forward, shaking Rachel's hand. "Great to meet you."

"You too," she replied with sincerity in her tone.

Lisa studied Rachel, then waved toward a table a few clusters over. "Well, we'll leave you two to enjoy your dinner."

"Find me later. I want to introduce you to someone." Mitch nodded

Now that was music to Hunter's ears. "Will do."

The Shaffers returned to their seats, and Hunter sat, replaced his napkin, and started on his cooling dinner. He noticed Rachel taking a few bites, but mostly she pushed her food around. The silence grew thick between them.

This had been a bad idea.

"Hunter," Rachel's soft voice broke his stream of thought. "I need to tell you something. I'm not who you think I am."

His brows pinched together. "You're not?"

She twisted her napkin in her lap. "I'm Rachel Johnson, but not *your* Rachel Johnson." Her cheeks tinted with pink. "I mean, not the Rachel I think you were looking for."

He set down his fork, turned to face her fully, and tried to hide how disappointed he felt about the evening.

Rachel worried her bottom lip. "When you came to Roger's office, and we met, I mean, I work for Roger. I was leaving for the day, saying goodbye, when you walked in." She blew out a breath and lowered her gaze. "God. I'm a bumbling fool," she muttered.

"No, you're not." Quite the opposite. She was stunning and graceful in her gown and heels.

She glanced up, blotting the corner of her lip with a napkin.

"So, you don't know Cheryl Moorland?"

She shook her head.

"And you don't actually work on the thirty-eighth floor for Watson, Bradley, and Chalmers?"

She fidgeted with the chain on her purse "No, I'm so sorry."

Hunter ran a hand through his hair. *Well, that explains a lot.*

What a cluster-fuck.

Still, he had no right to be mad at her, or Cheryl. He should be mad at himself. But why hadn't she said something?

She put her fingers on his forearm, pulling back quickly. "I tried to ask Roger about you, to return the invite, but he had to leave the country unexpectedly. Cell service is spotty in Sierra Leone. I had no way to contact you."

He was suddenly the embarrassed one. *He* had screwed this up, making assumptions. "Rachel, you're not the one who should be sorry. I am. I had every intention of seeing Rachel Johnson after dropping in on Roger. And when I heard him call your name...and your last name is Johnson?" What an odd coincidence.

She nodded. "It is. I only decided to come tonight because I thought it would be worse if I didn't. I mean, if you needed a date tonight, at least you wouldn't be left stranded." She plucked at the napkin in her lap. "I'll leave if you want."

Leave?

He stared at the beautiful profile of the woman next to

him. From the moment he'd laid eyes on her, he'd been enchanted. She might not be able to help him network, but he could certainly enjoy her company for the rest of the gala and salvage the evening. He was not one to mix business with women, but as she sat there, looking so positively stunning, he knew he had to make an exception.

He lifted her chin with a finger, turning so she could face him. "No, I don't want you to go."

"But your date, I mean..." Her voice trailed off.

"That was just a professional thing. That Rachel is supposedly well-connected. My best friend Ken's wife Cheryl normally accompanies me to these events, but she couldn't make it. She recommended I invite Rachel instead. It's all right that you're not her." His lips curved at the corners because he meant it. "That answers one of my questions—how you know Roger."

For as much as he was disappointed that she was the wrong woman, he was equally happy to be with her now.

Rachel exhaled. "So, this other Rachel was supposed to help you meet people?"

He smirked. "Yes. Well, the best laid plans..."

"You seem to have that under control." She flicked her eyes up to Leonard Smith, CEO of a small internet advertising company in serious growth-mode. Hunter hoped to make Leonard a customer.

Hunter rose and offered his hand. "Leonard, good evening."

They made introductions and polite chit chat before Leonard departed.

"That went well," he said.

"See?" She lifted her hand, palm up. "You know a lot of people already."

He grinned. "Touché."

After taking a bite of her tomato and mozzarella salad, she said, "I don't think we've had a proper introduction."

He extended his hand. "Hunter Baron. I own a small consulting firm. I specialize in helping companies in a state of extreme change. Glad to meet you."

She grinned. "Rachel Johnson. Administrative assistant to Roger Brennan, lover of wine, and keeper of the permanent markers."

He chuckled aloud. "You didn't mention a husband?"

"Only an ex." She sipped her wine. "And you? I assume no wife if you borrow your best friend's for corporate events," she said.

"Correct." He scooped in a bite full of rice, certainly not wanting to dive into the conversation of why right now.

Maybe the evening wasn't a complete loss. "Well, in spite of everything, I'm really glad you came tonight," he said sincerely.

Hunter didn't have much time for relationships. An occasional date, maybe with *dessert*, but nothing more. He usually had business on the brain when he attended these functions. This might be the first time he'd likely do very little business in exchange for enjoyment of a beautiful, single woman's company.

Frankly, no one could replace Jessica. What they'd had had been practically perfect and while he went out casually, he never encouraged a relationship.

He ate the last of his tenderloin and flagged down the waiter, turning to Rachel, "You said you love wine. Would you like red or white?"

"Chardonnay would be great."

He ordered two glasses of chardonnay to drink with the rest of their meal. He and Rachel chatted through the speech the executive director gave—nothing serious.

Rachel seemed to relax, like a weight had been lifted.

Cheryl would get a kick out of this mix-up, and Ken would probably razz him for years to come. Probably long after Rachel was out of the picture.

When they finished eating, a waitress refilled their wine glasses, and they strode to the silent auction tables. Rachel bid on a kids' birthday party for ten at some funhouse. Hunter bid on a few items—an autographed Babe Ruth baseball, a box at a Rockets game, and a jewelry gift certificate that Rachel oohed over. Hunter believed in giving back, even if he didn't win the item. Not only was it good for his broken soul, his bidding would drive up the price, thus helping the non-profit organization.

He managed to chat with a few more folks and got a card from the introduction Mitch made for him. His hand resting on Rachel's lower back as they walked the ballroom was incredibly comfortable.

The lights dimmed over the dance floor. Hunter glanced at his watch and was surprised to see that it was nearly eleven o'clock. The event was to end at midnight.

When the singer started an Ella Fitzgerald song, he reached for Rachel's hand. "Dance with me?"

The corners of her lips curled upward in delight. "I'd love to."

Rachel could breathe again. The lack of honesty had eaten at her. She prescribed to the belief that honesty was always the best policy. She'd been insanely nervous—forcing herself not to fidget with her dress—knowing full-well she had to tell Hunter he'd made a mistake. That it was a case of mistaken identity.

When she'd realized his date was for business purposes, her heart sank. Thankfully, Hunter didn't seem upset with her. Better still, he didn't want her to go home.

Instead, they'd chatted over dinner, and he met several people he knew.

When his friends, Mitch and Lisa, had stopped by, Rachel could instantly tell Lisa was disingenuous. She had a better-than-thou attitude with Rachel, but Rachel didn't care. That was Lisa's problem, not hers.

Some friends and customers introduced Hunter to new prospects. Rachel had seen Roger in action enough to know that people liked Hunter. He had a smooth confidence and seemed to take a genuine interest in their businesses.

Occasionally, Hunter's hand lingered on her lower back and Rachel loved it.

My goodness. She wore a formal dress at an elegant event and the most handsome man in the room was her date. Well, not exactly, but it sure felt that way.

His hands were warm, and unknowingly she had leaned in close to him. His rock-solid body was flush against the side of hers. Heat filled her cheeks when she'd realized what she was doing.

A quick trip to the ladies room helped her regain her composure. The thoughts about Hunter—his mouth, his hands, his strong body—distracted her. It was out of line when this was a business function to him.

Get it together, Rach.

Chapter Five

HUNTER ESCORTED RACHEL to the dance floor, finding a cozy spot amongst the crowd. His right hand wrapped around her waist, and her left draped over his strong shoulder.

He led effortlessly, like he'd danced a thousand times before. So unlike her ex who was awkward and self-conscience about people watching him dance. She couldn't remember when they'd last danced together.

She and Hunter moved in together as the singer's voice sent them on waves of melodious bliss. She couldn't have conjured up a better night in her fantasies. Hunter's charm was genuine and Rachel almost laughed out loud.

If Richie was being charming, it was a disguise for manipulation. It had taken Rachel a few years to figure that out.

As it had for Cinderella, she knew the night would soon come to an end. Until then, her friends had dressed her to the nines, her date was not only handsome, but an excellent dancer, and truthfully, it had been a long time since a man had held her like this.

And oh God, did Hunter hold her in just the right way, like she was special to him. When obviously that was impossible since they were mere strangers.

She would savor *every* moment.

One song flowed into the next, and Hunter pulled her closer, his shoulder muscles flexing under her touch. His subtle musk cologne tantalized her, dragging her farther into their dance.

His strong arm circled her, holding her as they moved about the dance floor. Her pulse sped and she willed herself to stay calm.

His warm breath caressed her cheek as he said softly, "You're an exceptional dancer."

She peered into his gorgeous rich chocolate eyes...the dim lights erased the hint of gray. "Thank you. I just want to let the music sweep me away."

The corners of his lids crinkled as he smiled. "Then it shall be," he whispered. "Close your eyes."

Her heart pounded like a drum but she did as he commanded and lowered her lashes. He tugged her closer, still in complete control. He wedged his leg between hers and moved them as one. They danced as if they were on air.

She felt an almost undetectable press of his semi-erect penis, causing her nipples to peak. If he danced this well, she could only imagine how he must be in bed. Those strong muscles and his gentle touch—she wanted to swoon. What she wouldn't give to see those muscles uncovered, in the flesh.

But that wasn't going to happen. She had two kids at home. One-night-stands were out of the question. And considering she'd likely never see this gorgeous man again, she'd tuck this memory away for her own private fantasy.

They floated over the dance floor. His leg pressed and scraped discreetly against her sex, building an exquisite ache deep inside. Rachel wished the night would never end.

"My friends." When the singer spoke she broke the spell and Rachel's breath hitched. She opened her eyes, glanced at Hunter, then the stage. Hunter steadied her.

"Folks, this will be the final dance of the night," the singer said. "Thank you so much for joining us in such a worthy cause. The silent auction is now closed. You can either stay and claim your goodies or you will receive a call to work out the arrangements later. Good evening, and we will see you next year."

The music started again, and the band closed with "Come Away With Me," one of Rachel's favorites.

They started to dance but with inches between them rather than thigh to thigh, and she wished they were closer.

"Rachel," he said low in her ear. "I don't regret inviting you tonight. I enjoyed myself immensely."

She met his gaze. "Thank you. I did, too."

They danced the remainder of the song in silence. She didn't want to ruin the moment, instead cherish every second before they had to leave.

The talented singer finished and Hunter and Rachel applauded with the remaining guests. The lights brightened. The magic vanished in a poof.

In the light, there were no pumpkins, but the space had definitely lost its luster. Dirty plates, crumpled napkins, and debris on the floor—all evidence of the end of a wonderful night.

"Do you want to see if you won anything in the silent auction?" she asked as they slowly treaded with the crowd off the dance floor.

"No, that's okay. If we won anything, they'll call us later. Do you have a coat?"

"Um, yes." She fished in her tiny clutch purse for the claim check and handed it to him.

He slipped the matching wrap over her shoulders and offered his arm to escort her to her car. The night—crisp and cool—enveloped them as they strode through the parking lot. The warmth from his touch coursing through her body kept the chilliness at bay.

"It seems rather ungentlemanly of me not to drive you home."

She glanced at him as they strolled, seeing a small twinkle even in the dark. Her lips curved slightly. He had a nice shape to his mouth, very kissable she was sure. "It's okay."

They reached her SUV and paused. He shoved his hands in his coat pockets in the chill of the January air. "Well, it was a happy coincidence that you have the same name as the woman I was supposed to ask to the Gala."

Rachel nodded. "Indeed. And again, I'm sorry." She would never regret it. It had been magical; the best night she'd had in a long time.

He shook his head. "You don't need to apologize."

Hunter stepped closer to her, her back against her vehicle, his beautiful gaze holding hers as he cupped her jaw with his hand and leaned down to graze his mouth over hers. She parted hers in invitation and he took more, skimming his tongue along her lower lip.

He dove fully into her mouth. Their lips meshed, tongues danced. The velvety strokes of his tongue elicited a sighing mewl from the back of her throat. His kiss took her to new heights, his lips smooth and firm.

How long had it been that she felt such an exquisite first kiss?

His left arm wrapped her closer into his hard body, leaving no space between them. The kiss wasn't just to satisfy his curiosity but for her pleasure as much as his.

His erection pressed into her, and the tension in her belly grew. Then, he pulled back, and a small puff of breath warmed her face. "I would love to call you sometime. May I?"

Her stomach flip-flopped at the notion. What about the

kids? She licked her lips, plowing ahead before she changed her mind. "Yes, that would be great."

There was a slight pause before his lips curved. His smile made her want more kisses, more of everything.

He opened the door of her SUV. She slid in, and he helped tuck in her gown safely.

"Goodnight."

"Goodnight." He pushed the door closed and waved at her through the glass window.

"A good night indeed," she whispered to herself as he strolled toward his imported car. "Wow."

Hunter turned his head one last time to watch Rachel drive away in her SUV. He had no words to express how he felt about the night. At first, frustration had ruled as he realized that his plans for networking and making new contacts had gone to shit. Then Rachel admitted that she'd been the wrong Rachel. She'd said she was sorry. *She* was sorry. This had been all his fault. He'd jumped to conclusions, just hearing her name and seeing her leave Roger's office. He was the one who should be sorry.

But it all made total sense—why she'd been hesitant, almost skittish. How could he be mad? So things hadn't gone as he'd expected and he'd had no choice but to make the best of it.

And did he receive the best in return, or what?

Rachel was a surprisingly authentic woman. Her

glowing smile, twinkling eyes, and lavish curves coupled with her forthright nature absolutely threw him for a loop. Holding her close—so close, he thought for sure she'd slap him—made him want to do so many more things with her. Starting with no audience, and no dress.

God, she was beautiful. Hunter had noticed the glimpses from other men at the Gala, and was grateful the roles weren't reversed. She was *his* date for the night. If the music hadn't stopped, he would still be holding her close, dancing. And in all honesty, if he didn't have to go to San Antonio first thing in the morning, he would have asked her back to his place. For more dancing. He'd strip that gown off that delectable body and dive into what was hidden underneath.

He groaned at the red light and adjusted his pants to accommodate a fierce hard-on. He would need to fix that when he got home.

Just the thought of being alone with Rachel wound him up. When was the last time a woman had energized him like this? Not since Jessica, but he forced that thought down because all too often the pain that bubbled up ruined any good feelings he had.

~

Friday over breakfast, Rachel still glowed from the magical night she'd had with the mystery man Hunter. She was unbelievably thankful that she'd gone.

She'd told the kids it was sort of a work function, so that morning they hadn't mentioned a thing, but it was all Rachel could think about.

"Okay, kids, grab your backpacks. We gotta go."

She dropped off the kids on time and made it to work to find Roger at his computer, a deep crease in his forehead.

"Hey, Rachel. Glad you're here." He held up a sheet of paper.

She hustled into his office to take it and scan it. It mentioned something about recycled earth elements and then listed a few company names.

"Would you mind searching up the contact info for those companies, typing it up and sending it to me?" He met her gaze head-on. "I'll tell you what, we're gonna find another source for the rare earth elements, to the extent that we can. I'm not keeping our eggs in one basket any longer," he said with determination in his voice.

"You got it, boss. And I'm glad your back."

He smiled.

As she worked on the memo for Roger, Rachel glanced at her ringing cell phone. *Alexis.*

"Hey."

"How come I didn't hear from you last night?" Lexi demanded without bothering with *hello.*

"I didn't get home until after midnight."

"Excuse me? Miss Prim and Proper? Mother of two so I can't have fun anymore, didn't get home until after midnight?

Goodness, I better sit down.”

Rachel had to laugh. It might be true, so she wasn't the least bit offended. “I had such an amazing time.”

“Tell me all about it.”

“The event was spectacular—the food, the band, the dancing.” She sighed. “Hunter's a wonderful dancer.”

“Oh yeah? And what else? He wasn't mad, was he?”

Rachel had been nervous from the moment she'd slipped on her gown that she'd made a mistake trying to save him from being solo at the Gala. Thank the stars above that it hadn't ruined the night when she'd finally confessed. “No, he wasn't mad. It was supposed to be a business date, like a networking thing.”

“Really?” Lexi's voice pitched higher with surprise.

“Yeah. I thought for sure that he'd want to call it a night once I was able to explain the mix-up—but we talked. We danced. What a wonderful dancer...” She'd already downloaded a few Tina Turner songs she didn't have on her phone.

“Yeah, I got that.”

“And then we kissed.” *And my, what a kiss it was.*

“Okay, now it's gettin' good. What else?”

“Alexis! I'm not that kinda girl.”

“You used to be.”

Lexi was mostly right. During college and definitely before having kids, Rachel's life could be characterized as colorful.

"Not exactly, but nevertheless, I have kids to bear in mind."

Lexi let out an exasperated sigh. "Not a good excuse. You're allowed to move on. You're allowed to date."

"Well, we'll see. He asked if he could call me. Things might grind to a halt after I tell him I have two kids at home."

"He'll love the kids, too. Don't worry. I gotta get back to work. Let's talk later."

"Okay. I'll get the dress cleaned. And thanks again for making me go."

Alexis chuckled. "Always welcome."

The line went dead. She smiled for a bit longer. If Hunter did call, and they did go out, and he didn't have an issue with kids, well, then, she might just owe Alexis more than a *thank you.*

But that was a lot of *ifs.*

The smile Rachel wore most of the day began to fade. It was after five o'clock, with no word from Hunter, and staring at the phone wouldn't make it ring.

"Hey. Aren't you heading out?" Roger waited at the entrance to her cubicle, fishing the keys from his jacket pocket.

"Yeah, I'm just wrapping it up." *Stalling is more like it.*

Roger hovered like he wanted to ask her something. "Okay. Next week we can finalize the anniversary party details."

"Sounds good."

"Well, have a great weekend," Roger called as he strode to the bank of elevators.

"You, too."

She double-checked her calendar for Monday then began shutting down her PC. She retrieved her purse and rifled through for some lip balm, tossing away old receipts in the process.

Why didn't I think to give him my cell number?

Rachel stood to straighten her files, notepad, and pens. She could wipe down her desk, but that would mean going to the breakroom for cleaner and a cloth. She should just go home.

She looked up at nothing and exhaled. No sense delaying anymore. Hunter probably got crazy busy and would call her Monday, unless he found some magical way to get her home number. *Unrealistic, Rachel.*

Rachel grabbed her coat as she headed out and crossed her fingers that Hunter would call her soon.

Two weeks passed with no call from Hunter. Rachel was such a fool to think they had shared a moment. *What moment? There was no damn moment.*

Maybe he'd thought he could get her into bed. Or maybe he'd learned that someone important had been at the Gala and he'd missed the opportunity to meet them because of the mix-up.

Rachel filled her days with final preparations for the

company's ten-year anniversary in a few days, in addition to her usual tasks. She'd confirmed with Bethany that it would likely be a late night. Roger had asked her several times if everything was all right. She brushed it off, but dammit, she needed to get her act together. This job was too important to risk.

She was clearly a passing fancy to Hunter. A kiss at midnight.

Chapter Six

HUNTER CHATTED WITH a few people, mostly Roger's employees, at the back of the hotel ballroom. When Roger had invited him to the company's ten-year anniversary party, he'd jumped on it. Hunter knew this was probably matchmaking on Roger's part, but he'd take it. He'd been an ass for not calling Rachel. This was a golden opportunity to speak to her and make things right. Maybe, just maybe, she'd find it in her heart to forgive him and let him take her out.

Rachel walked gracefully onto the dais and handed Roger the microphone. She said a few words to him, a beautiful smile on her face, and then stepped back. In her fitted black pants and heels with her purple silk blouse, she looked the epitome of a confident professional.

Roger tapped the mic and drew everyone's attention. He beamed. "Evening folks, this is a major milestone. You should congratulate yourselves. These first ten years have been amazing. We've grown from a small company with one office and one tiny warehouse to a mid-size company, and we're getting bigger every year." He reached for a flute of champagne from the server's tray. "If you would all grab a glass of bubbly, I would like to make a toast. To the finest bunch of people I have ever had the privilege to work with. Here's to ten more years. Here's to a successful future."

"Here, here," someone cheered.

After the toast, Hunter wend through the crowd toward the stage where he'd last seen Rachel, but she was no longer there. He spun around, scanning the room. *She was right here.*

He searched and mingled, finally deciding to grab a plate of appetizers at the buffet table and refill his wine glass. After several minutes, he spotted Rachel talking with a group of women in front of the chocolate fountain. He quickly set his dish on a nearby table and made a beeline to her.

"Hello, Rachel."

She twisted to her right and gave him a small smile. "Hi. I didn't know you were here."

"Roger invited me a few days ago. I was hoping to see you here tonight."

"Oh yeah?" Her smile disappeared and her face became neutral, completely unreadable.

Just then a twenty-something man approached, his eyes wide with panic. He leaned close to her ear. "There's a problem with the cake."

"Okay, I'll be right there." She directed her gaze to

Hunter. "Sorry, hold that thought. I'll be back in just a minute." She held up her index finger, then turned to leave the ballroom.

Patience. He knew the blame for this fell on his shoulders. Of course, she'd be more apt to give him the brush off—he said he'd call and he hadn't.

A minute turned into twenty. Hunter wasn't having much success in getting a private conversation with Rachel. He scrubbed a hand over his jaw. He realized she was being pulled in a million directions and fate was not in his corner.

Hunter had just finished his dinner, sitting at a large round table with some of Roger's executives, when he caught Rachel's eye from several feet away.

Rachel gave him a tentative smile as she approached him. "So sorry about that. Some days it seems like my work is never done." She pushed a blonde lock of hair off her face.

He rose. He had the distinct impression she was very much the backbone of this company, and he admired her for it. He also wondered how much she'd intentionally avoided him. And his chest ached a little at the thought. "I can see that. There is no need to apologize. I owe *you* an apology. I had to leave town the day after the Gala and things did not go as well as I'd planned."

Rachel's smooth brow furrowed. "Oh." She glanced down at her shoes, then back at him. "I thought you might be mad about the identity fiasco."

He reached for her hand. "No. The mix-up was all my

fault. I was hoping I would see you here. You're the main reason I came tonight."

"Really?"

He nodded and shifted closer. "I should have called you, but I only had your office number, which limited when I could call. And it occurred to me you might have a boyfriend, and then so much time had passed..." He trailed off because he knew he'd been an ass and trying to articulate a decent apology was harder than he thought.

She squeezed his fingers. "It's alright. I'm glad you're here now. And no, I don't have a boyfriend."

He allowed a slow smile to form. That was good news, that was progress.

"There is an ex-husband," she continued. "We've been officially divorced one year now." She blinked. "I got the house and two wonderful children out of the deal."

Kids? He did his damnedest to keep his surprise to himself.

He recalled several conversations with Jessica about children of their own. They were career-minded and thought they had more time. They were wrong.

Kids should certainly be expected when she'd been married before. Again, not that it mattered. Did it?

Wasn't there some sort of rule about dating single moms?

Fuck!

A blush crept over Rachel's cheeks and she glanced

away. "Look, I need to get back to the kitchen and check on things."

He was such an ass. His throat grew thick with embarrassment, but he didn't know how to recover. She turned and quickly dashed from the ballroom out a side door.

Double fuck!

Could he screw this up any worse? First of all, he scolded himself, it doesn't matter if she has kids. That shouldn't change the fact that they could go on a few dates, share companionship for a short time. *Secondly, don't make her feel bad about it.* Pull your head out of your ass and make this right, he scolded himself.

He wiped the beads of sweat that had gathered on his brow. He needed a miracle. The butterfly garden popped in his head.

Yes! He texted Billy, praying the man worked tonight.

He started for the door Rachel had walked through when Roger approached him.

"Buddy, I'm glad you could make it," Roger said with a slight slur, taking Hunter in a bear hug and slapping him on the back.

"Wouldn't miss it for the world. I'm happy for you and all your success."

Beth sidled up next to her husband. "There you are." She wore a long black dress and had her brown wavy hair pulled back to show off her sparkling dangly earrings.

"Hey, babe." Roger smacked a loud kiss over her lips.

Smiling, Beth glanced up at Hunter. "Hey, Hunter. Good to see you. It's been a while."

He hugged her and kissed her cheek. "Good to see you, too. You look great. Yes, I've been busy with work, but I'm not complaining."

"My husband is having himself a really good time tonight."

Hunter covered a surprised laugh with a cough. "Indeed."

Hunter wouldn't fault him. Roger was never a heavy drinker, even through college. But to celebrate the success of a company he'd started with his own bare hands, no one would dare criticize.

"Babe, I'm having the *best* time." Roger wrapped his arms around her waist. "Want to take this party home?" He wiggled his eyebrows and gave her a licentious grin.

Beth swatted his chest. "Oh, you're so bad," but the twinkle in her eye told another story.

"Hunter, before I f'get. Have you met my assistant, Rachel? She's da' best. She was lookin' fer you while I was in Sierra Leone." He winked, not so subtly, and Hunter chuckled.

"Yes. I have. Thanks for telling me." Of course, she had been. She'd been trying to give back the invitation he'd so foolishly thought was to go to her.

"C'mon, my drunken man. Let me get you home to bed."

"Baby, das music to my ears." Roger looped his arm over

her shoulder, and they made their way to the door, hip to hip.

Hunter watched them leave and squelched the feeling he'd once had of having someone in his life to rely on.

He refocused. He had to find Rachel and try to dislodge the foot that seemed to keep landing in his mouth.

Rachel had managed to avoid Hunter for the past hour and discreetly said her goodbyes. She'd been furious with herself for days, hoping he'd call. Then the first thing she'd wanted to do when she saw him was hide away to get more of his kisses. Those spectacular kisses...

She'd made it through the hotel door to the parking lot when she heard Hunter call her name.

"Rachel?"

She wasn't naïve. Men like Hunter didn't want women with baggage. Who could blame him? But frankly, she didn't have time for this. She loved her kids and was proud of them. She wouldn't dodge around it or make excuses.

Forget that Hunter was attractive, or a good dancer, or a great kisser. Forget that somewhere deep inside she ached for a man to hold her naked body, kiss her until her lips were raw, or make love to her until the sun came up.

Richie never did that.

If Hunter wasn't the one, she would accept it and keep looking. She'd thought he was an impressive gentleman, and that they had chemistry, but now, she wasn't so sure.

Halfway to her car in the parking lot, she stopped and

turned to face him. "Look, it's okay, Hunter. I know a single mom with kids isn't what you'd banked on." Something dark flashed in his eyes, but Rachel had to say her piece so they could end this flirtation. This relationship, if she could even call it that, was clearly doomed for failure before it even started. "I don't expect anything from you. I had a great time at the Gala, and I know there's nothing in the cards for us. That's all right. Take care." She waved goodbye and hurried toward her SUV. All this thinking about Hunter, talking to him, not talking to him, was going to give her an ulcer. Some days she wished she'd never met the man. *Dammit!*

His footsteps sounded behind her. "Wait. Please. Can we go somewhere to talk?"

She spun around, meeting his stare dead-on. "What?"

"Let me take you somewhere."

Was he serious? "Now?"

"Yeah. I won't keep you out long. I promise. Are the kids with a sitter or their dad?"

She pursed her lips. Bethany already knew this would be a late night, so that wasn't a concern. But was he worth the headache? Should she go with him and risk more of the yo-yo feeling she'd been having for weeks now?

She could see he was making an effort.

In all honesty, never in her life had someone made her ache with longing. Not like Hunter had. Her job and being a mom were fulfilling, but they weren't *everything*.

Ah, hell. "Okay. But not too late."

His beautiful smile flashed a mix of triumph with relief. "My car is right over here." He stretched out his arm, and she allowed his free hand to rest on her lower back as they walked. How she missed the feeling of a man's strong, warm hand guiding her.

He drove them outside the city in the direction of the zoo. She knew it well because of several trips she'd taken with the kids. Although, the zoo was closed at this late hour.

After a few minutes, Hunter broke the heavy silence in the car. "You were very busy tonight. Does Roger keep you hopping?"

She didn't know how to respond to that. Was he being critical of Roger or just making small talk? "I was busy. It's not so much Roger's doing as my own. I like to keep things running smoothly. It's in my nature."

His left hand rested on the wheel as his right cupped the gear shift. "Well, you did a great job. The event was wonderful."

"Thanks." The leather in his car felt soft. She shifted to face him slightly. "How do you know Roger?"

A small smile appeared. "We roomed together for two years in college, then I moved off-campus in an apartment, and he moved into a frat house. We stayed in touch. He's a good man."

She knew that he was, and he'd worked hard for his success. "Yes, and a good boss."

"I'm glad to hear that." Hunter cleared his throat.

"Rachel, I owe you an apology. Again. I didn't mean to react the way I did when you told me you have kids."

She kept her attention on the road ahead of them. Her face grew warm, which made her defensive...she had nothing to be embarrassed about.

"I like you. I like spending time with you," he continued. "It makes perfect sense that you would have kids, and I bet you're a great mom. Please don't let my foolishness get in the way of us getting to know each other."

She turned to face him, and the sincerity in his voice thawed her toward him. Having some adult-time, alone time with a man, appealed to Rachel in ways she didn't fully understand herself. Just the thought of his kisses brought her senses alive.

That's a pretty good apology, she thought. She still wondered what he wanted. Of course, having asked the question meant she already knew the answer. "Okay. We can try again."

"Good." He smiled. "I want to make it up to you. Bring you somewhere special." He steered the car into the parking lot of the Cockrell Butterfly Center. She'd heard about this place, but never had a chance to visit.

But... "Isn't it closed now?"

Hunter grinned so adorably her stomach did somersaults. "Officially, yes." He unbuckled his seatbelt to face her. "I actually did some work for the Center a few years ago. They also hosted a community volunteer outreach, so I pitched in. The security guard knows me well. C'mon."

He quickly exited the car, and went to her side, guiding her hand-in-hand as they approached the front door of the three-story glass building.

Rachel held her coat closed as they watched a guard cross the lobby toward the massive front door and unlock it. "Evening, Mr. Baron."

Hunter held the door for her. "Good evening, Billy. May I introduce Rachel Johnson?"

"Evening, Ms. Johnson."

The guard stood about five-eleven, had smooth dark skin, and a navy uniform that contrasted against his brilliant smile.

She nodded. "Nice to meet you."

Billy looked at Hunter. "I turned the lights on low. Take as much time as you'd like." His eyes twinkled as he ushered them inside then closed and locked up behind them.

"I can't wait to show you," Hunter said, escorting her farther into the building and through a glass door.

Her heels clicked against the tile floor making the only sound in the place. "Hunter, are we allowed to be here?" Her stomach knotted tighter with every step they took. She glanced over her shoulder. Being arrested for trespassing was not her idea of fun.

Holding her hand, he pecked a kiss to the tip of her nose. "It's alright. Billy practically runs the place. It'll be great. I promise."

They passed through a final glass door into the butterfly conservatory—a tall, open space with nothing but foliage and butterflies freely flying about. Lots of butterflies in every imaginable color. Her jaw hung open in wonder. "Wow," she breathed.

He slowly led her farther in, the peaceful sounds of nature like a soundtrack. "Is that a waterfall I hear?"

He nodded. "Thirty feet tall. There are sixty different varieties of butterflies in here."

"How do you know all this?"

"I studied up when I was hired to work for them a few years back. I try to learn all I can about my clients. Fascinating, isn't it?"

Her gaze traveled up, up, to the glass ceiling of the indoor rainforest, softly lit in the darkness surrounding them. Hundreds of live butterflies flitted about, dancing and swirling, without a care in the world.

They followed the paths deeper into the structure, meandering through the exotic plants that enveloped them. After several minutes, they stopped in front of the rushing waterfall. She gasped. "Amazing."

"Truly." He pivoted toward her as if they were on the dance floor, mere inches between them. "It's even better in the daylight, but I wanted to bring you here tonight. Just the two of us." He cupped her face, running his thumb over her cheek, causing her heart to beat as rapidly as the water falling into the pond below it. "Please forgive me for acting like such an ass," he whispered. His eyes darkened, holding her gaze, and at that moment, she could kiss him.

Hunter understood that Rachel was about done with him and he needed to make it up to her. He didn't know why he felt the compulsion to make things right. He had half a mind to just throw in the towel and leave the woman alone. But that was just it—he couldn't. Hell, he was just as confused as she. From the moment she'd run into him outside Roger's office, he couldn't forget her.

"Okay," she whispered, her sweet breath caressing his face.

With that, he knew he had a small chance to win her over. And he couldn't ask for a more secluded spot to be alone, if only for several minutes.

Hunter stepped closer, his body flush against hers. Rachel tipped her head up to meet his gaze. He couldn't resist her full lips. He leaned down and brushed his lips over hers. He nibbled and as her lips parted, he slowly reached his tongue to find hers welcoming. He caressed and stroked her tongue with his, eliciting a soft moan.

He cupped the back of her neck with his left hand and slid his right gently down her throat. He broke the kiss and stared down her, running his thumb over her smooth bottom lip. Her mouth slightly gaped in desire.

"You are so beautiful."

He dove into her sweet mouth again, swallowing her

mewls, one after the other. He wanted more. How far could he take it in this private-yet-public setting?

Her arms looped around his neck, inviting him to pull her closer.

His left arm wrapped her waist, holding her as he pushed a leg between her thighs, wanting so much to hear her moans and soft cries that he'd touch anywhere she'd allow.

His hand glossed down her throat to the V in her blouse. His knuckles brushed her skin and the top of her cleavage, which pushed against the lapels of her coat.

Christ, he wanted her more than he'd wanted another woman in a long time. And it scared the shit out of him, but he would deal with the guilt later.

She tore her mouth from his, panting. "Hunter," she breathed out.

He loved hearing her say his name—it only confirmed she wanted him to continue.

He kissed the side of her mouth, her cheek, and as her head tipped backward, he claimed her neck, tasting, kissing, sucking her sweet skin.

With steady fingers, he slipped open several buttons of her blouse.

"Hunter." Her hand covered his.

He held her gaze, wondering if he should tell her they were all alone.

She smoothed her lips together as if debating her next move, then she lowered her hand to her side.

Thank the heavens above, he could continue. He gently pushed aside the fabric of her jacket, then her shirt, allowing him to caress her full breasts. She sighed.

Would she let him taste?

He grazed a fingertip along the lace of her bra, up and down, waiting for her opposition, praying it wouldn't come. His ministrations peaked both nipples, practically begging him for more. He shifted his leg gently against the apex of her thighs. She gasped and it spurred him on. The erection in his pants was solid granite.

His finger slipped under the lacy confection, drawing the fabric down one breast as he wasted no time claiming her pointed nipple. With his tongue, he toyed and sucked while his hand cupped and massaged her soft breast.

Her fingers wove through his hair gently tugging with each erotic wave she rode.

He exposed her other breast and quickly sucked her nipple into his mouth, soon opening wider to take in as much as he could. She moaned louder.

As he tasted her warm, luscious breasts, his thigh had a mind of its own—swaying to and fro, caressing her warm sex, eager to bring her to climax.

"Hunter," she pleaded. "You have to stop. I... I might come like this."

He looked her square in her glassy eyes. "I want you to," he breathed over her breast before he took it again, sucking harder.

She shrieked and her hips jolted against him. Her hands gripped his shoulders.

He held her tight, pulling her, rocking her against him, urging this incredible woman to seek the pleasure she so richly deserved. If he had his way, there would be more opportunities to bring her joy, over and over.

Her breathing sped, and his mouth moved to her right breast as his fingers toyed with the nipple of the other.

She lifted her knee, improving the angle of friction against him.

That's right, beautiful.

"Oh, God. Hunter." She tugged his hair—a delicious sting shooting through his scalp—while she rocked her hips harder and faster. "Oh God." She moaned long and low, and he glanced upward to see an expression of ecstasy.

Slowly, her eyes opened and the grip on his hair loosened. "Oh wow," she whispered, her face flushed with her impetuous climax.

He wrapped both arms around her, closing the gap between them, and kissed her, pouring out all his passion for her. He ached to be inside her, but he knew it had to wait. This was about her. The perfect time would come, and he would make damn sure it was good for her then too.

Hunter drove Rachel back to the hotel, the parking lot largely cleared out at this hour after the party. Embarrassed, she'd hardly peeked his way the entire drive. Her behavior at the butterfly museum mortified her. Never before had she lost control, certainly never with Richie.

"What are you thinking?" He broke her stream of thought as he stopped his car alongside her SUV.

She smoothed her lips together, inhaling a breath through her nose, then exhaling. "I can't believe what I did in the butterfly garden."

"Ah. I thought you were quiet. Please look at me, Rachel."

She turned to face Hunter, and he cupped his hand over hers resting on her lap.

"I love what *we* did. I'm sorry if I took it too far. I am. But I promise you, no one saw. It doesn't change how I think about you."

"Well, it should," she whispered and glanced down. "That was the first time I've done something like that with someone not my husband." But more importantly, she was an adult. She should know doing something like that in public was risky.

"You are too hard on yourself." His finger lifted her chin back to meet his gaze. "What happened we *both* did. We both liked it. And I'd really like to see you again."

Her body said *Yes*, but her brain said *No. Tell him to take a hike.*

She could keep it physical. That's what he wanted, and God, how she wanted some of that too. She could be careful to protect her heart and shield this from the kids. She and

Hunter could have some fun for a while, and then move on, right?

The memory of his kisses, his touch, had her speaking before she thought wiser. "Okay."

He smiled and squeezed her hand. "How is Saturday night?"

"Um, can't. I have the kids. But I'm open the next Friday." For a split second, she thought about inviting him to her birthday dinner, but with the night's plans uncertain, she opted to keep the evening with her girlfriends.

"Perfect." He leaned closer and placed a simple, warm kiss on her lips, then pulled back. "Next Friday it is."

She fished out a piece of paper and a pen from her purse. *I shouldn't be doing this.* "Here is my cell phone and my address." She handed him the paper. With a small smile she replied, "See you in two weeks."

She looped her purse over her shoulder and opened his car door.

"I can't wait. G'night, Rachel."

"Goodnight, Hunter." She pushed the door closed and climbed into her SUV.

Two weeks. She couldn't wait either. She shouldn't be so giddy about it; Hunter was liable to just break her heart. She would protect it. But she wondered if this was how it would be—dates every other weekend when she didn't have the kids.

Doesn't matter, she told herself. *Enjoy it while it lasts.*

Chapter Seven

CHERYL MOORLAND'S NUMBER lit up his cell phone Tuesday morning on his way to the office. In the recent confusion—with a healthy dose of intrigue—Hunter had forgotten to circle back with her. Inside, he could admit he was embarrassed by the whole incident with Rachel because it was entirely his fault.

"Cheryl, how you feeling?" he answered.

"I'm better, one hundred percent. And Ken's glad to have me cooking again." She laughed at her own joke, and Hunter chuckled. "Anyway, what the heck happened? Did you go to the Gala? Rachel said she never heard from you."

"Uh, funny thing about that." He rubbed his knuckles against his jaw. "You won't believe me, but here goes. I was on the way to Rachel's office in the Palladium building to give her the invite but stopped on the sixteenth floor to see an old friend. A woman was leaving his office and her name was Rachel Johnson. Not knowing what your friend looked like, I assumed it was the same person. I was wrong.”

“Ohmigod, you’re kidding. So let me guess? You invited her, and she accepted.”

“Not exactly. I didn’t give her much chance to say no, but like I said, it worked out great in the end.” More than great. Running into Rachel had been the highlight to his month.

“Really? Okay, good.” There was a slight pause on the line, then, “So, it worked out great, how…? Do you like this Rachel?”

The words stuck in his throat and he couldn’t answer immediately. He did like her, and part of him ached that he might be dishonoring the memory of his wife.

He swallowed. “I do like her. We’ll see.”

“Good, Hunter. I can’t tell you how happy I am to hear that. Give this woman a chance, will ya? Enough time has passed. You’re allowed to move on.”

He pinched the bridge of his nose.

“Now, I’m supposed to remind you that Ken moved squash to Sunday, and you need to bring your A-game.”

He smirked. “Tell him I’ll be ready, and what I’ll bring is BENGAY because I know he’ll need it.”

The conversation wrapped up in a few short minutes. The talk of Rachel brought her smile to mind. He thought of where he should take her on their upcoming date. He knew several great restaurants but he wanted something more unique, more memorable.

But there was one thing he'd play be ear. As much as he craved touching her and bringing her to the ultimate in pleasure, could he exercise some restraint?

What happened in the butterfly garden was audacious and inexcusable, not to mention insane. She deserved better than that.

Showing her a special, memorable time was top priority. The sex, as much as he wanted it, he'd make a decision when the time came.

Then an idea popped in his head of the perfect date. His lips curved. It was perfect.

~

Tuesday night, Rachel lifted the lid off the pasta primavera, the aroma of tomato and spices filling her nostrils. She was stirring when her cell phone rang from its place on the kitchen counter. She hoped it was Hunter, although she knew he traveled for his business. She flipped her phone over.

Richie. She answered the phone with her free hand. "Hello."

"Rachel, I need to pick the kids up right after school Friday." Her ex didn't bother with hello. "Can you have them ready?" It wasn't the words so much as how he asked. Like she wasn't capable of making it happen.

She rolled her eyes. "Sure. Also, this Saturday is Brittany's birthday party and sleepover. Violet should be there around five o'clock. She'll have a wrapped present with her."

"Wait a minute. It's a sleepover?" Richie's voice took on an edge.

"Yes." *What's the big deal?*

"I didn't know that. I don't like it."

She sighed. "Why not? She's been on sleepovers before, Richie."

"No. Not a girl eleven, almost twelve. They'll sneak out."

She squinted her eyes, gripping the spoon tighter as she stirred faster. "What? They don't sneak out."

"They do, Rachel. They'll meet boys and whatever. And our daughter will not be partaking."

Rachel unclenched her jaw with difficulty. "Richie, she's been looking forward to this for weeks. We need to trust her."

"I trust her, but not the other girls. Just tell her I'll be picking her up from Brittany's at ten o'clock. No sleepover."

She drew in a calming breath, reigning in her desire to argue; it had always gotten them nowhere. "I think you're being unreasonable, but if you feel that strongly about it, *you* tell her."

He huffed over the line. "Fine. I'll be there Friday afternoon. Have them ready."

The line went dead.

Rachel glared at the phone. That was just like him—to be judgmental and steamroll over her assuming his way was always right.

Then, he'd expect her to deliver the bad news because he wouldn't do it and be labeled the bad guy. He was a good father, she knew, but she would not be his scapegoat.

She scoffed while she tapped the spoon against the side and covered her pot, then wiped her sweaty palm against her jeans.

She'd divorced this man because she couldn't stand him anymore, couldn't stand his controlling her. And she *hated* that he was still in her life. Her two wonderful kids were the only good thing to come out of that thirteen-year marriage. Good luck to the woman he was dating now.

Rachel shook her head and stared at the wall but there were no answers to be found. He frustrated her almost every time they spoke. Alexis had encouraged her to stand up to him, but it would do no good. It was just easier to concede and get him off the phone as soon as possible.

But damn if there weren't days she wished he'd just get hit by a bus.

Before her thoughts could run away any further, her doorbell rang. She checked the clock on the stove. Perfect timing. She opened the door.

Lexi stood before her in black boots, a straight skirt, and a fitted leather jacket, having come to dinner right from work. "Hey, *chica*."

She hugged her friend. "Hey."

Gripping her shoulders, Lexi leaned back to study Rachel's face. "What's wrong?"

Rachel sighed. "Just got off the phone with Richie. He's being an A-hole, that's all." She pushed the door closed behind her friend and dragged her toward the kitchen.

"Ah, typical. But you know what I always say: happiness is the best revenge. So, let's figure out what you should wear for your hot date."

Rachel smiled. Thoughts of Hunter usually made her happy. She had a big weekend coming up with her date and then her birthday party, so Lexi's input was invaluable. "Okay, but dinner first. And don't let me forget to give you back the gown and accessories." She walked to the bottom of the steps and called out, "Kids. Dinner. Wash up."

"What are we having? It smells good." Lexi followed her toward the stove and lifted the lid on the pot.

"Pasta primavera."

"Yum."

The four sat down at the round table and began to eat. The kids enjoying their time with "Aunt Lexi".

"Aunt Lexi, what did one wall say to the other wall?" Ethan asked.

"I don't know. What did one wall say to the other wall?"

"I'll meet you at the corner."

The kids giggled out loud, and the women smiled.

"What do you call a pig that knows karate?" Violet joined in on the fun.

Lexi grinned and shook her head.

"A pork chop!"

They all laughed. The kids loved to make their Aunt Lexi laugh.

"Okay. My turn." Lexi sipped her water. "How do the oceans say hello to each other?"

The kids replied in unison, "They wave!"

More belly laughs from around the table—these were the times Rachel lived for.

After cleaning up from dinner, the women went to her closet to make some selections for what she could wear on her upcoming date.

"Rach, you need more color in your wardrobe," Lexi stated, staring at her closet with her arms crossed in front of her.

"I have color. Look, I have ivory, off-white, eggshell, ecru—"

Alexis raised her hand. "Doesn't count. You need something off the *color wheel*." She emphasized the last two words.

Alexis was right. Rachel used to have color, as a kid, throughout college, even the first few years of marriage. She'd worn color and surrounded herself with bright hues—like standing in the middle of a butterfly garden. She almost chuckled. Somewhere along the way that spark had fizzled out as she'd settled down. She sighed. "What do I do?"

Alexis closed the closet door. "We go shopping, of course."

The following night, Rachel found herself in the women's dress department at the Houston Galleria Mall. She glanced down at the load of colorful clothes draped over her arm. "I really don't think I need anymore, Lexi."

"Yes, you do. Plus, you should get something for your birthday dinner. You deserve it." Alexis waggled her eyebrows and held up a red, scoop-neck dress in front of Rachel. With another waggle, she slung it over her arm, the pile growing bigger by the minute. "When was the last time you bought clothes for yourself?"

"I ordered some workout stuff online last week."

Lexi tilted her head and frowned. "Not what I had in mind."

"May I place those in dressing rooms for you ladies?" a voice asked from behind.

Rachel pivoted to see a twenty-something saleswoman with flawless cocoa skin and a chic short hairstyle smiling at them.

"Yes, please. We can share." Lexi handed off the mountain of clothes, and God bless the saleswoman, because she took Rachel's stack as well.

Lexi grabbed four more dresses, and they made it to a large dressing room.

Rachel plopped her butt on the bench.

"Don't poop out on me yet. After this, we can get dinner." Lexi pulled a lilac silk blouse off its hanger. "And drinks!"

An hour later, Rachel had the beginnings of a new wardrobe. She had to admit, she looked good in colors other than tan, beige, taupe, and brown.

"So the date is Friday?"

"Uh-huh."

"Do you know where he's taking you?"

"Nope, but after the whole butterfly garden trip, I'm sure I'll like it." Thoughts of that night still had Rachel clenching her legs together. What they'd done had been pure craziness—a part of her would do it all over again.

After checking out and hefting the bags full of clothes—four dresses, five blouses, two sweaters, two skirts, and one pair slacks—into the back of her SUV, they headed to a local Tex-Mex restaurant and ordered food.

Rachel speared a cucumber slice off her steak salad. "I think we need to talk about *you* going on a date, Lex. When was the last time a man took you out?"

Lexi shook her head. "Hell no. Men are too much damn work. Their sensitive egos, their fixation with sports," she waved a hand and leaned in, "having no clue how to get me off. Who needs it?"

Rachel bit back a laugh. "I think you're turning cynical in your old age, Ms. King. What happened to your expert man-advice? 'You gotta go into it like me—to have fun.'"

Lexi stopped mid-bite. "Wait a minute. Is that what you're doing with Hunter? You don't think this is more than just sex?"

Rachel scanned the restaurant to make sure no one was listening. "I seriously doubt he thinks of me as anything more than a good time for a while." She leaned in closer. "But ya know, I'm okay with that."

"It makes me wonder, if he's such a catch, how come he isn't married?"

Rachel had wondered that herself but hadn't had the chance to ask him. The timing never seemed right. "I don't know. Maybe I'll find out on Friday."

"Good thinking. Next, since you have a sitter tonight, we should go see a movie."

"Yes, I want to see that new chick-flick."

Lexi grinned. "I knew you would."

Chapter Eight

HUNTER SHOVED HIS toiletry bag in his suitcase. *All this travel is getting old.*

This trip to Dallas was to meet with Zeo Incorporated, one of the fastest growing app development companies in the nation. Hunter loved his company and connecting with people...staying busy kept his mind off the might-have-beens. The travel—that was another story. He frequented some of the same hotels so often that he was starting to recognize the hotel employees. He had to chuckle. *This is what a successful business looks like.*

More and more his mind wandered to Rachel. Traveling not only meant strange beds, but it meant less time to be able to see her. How could he take her on a date when he was constantly gone? The road travel will settle down soon, he told himself.

She probably had a happy routine with her kids and she certainly didn't need her life screwed up by men floating in and out of it. But damn, they could share a few dates, a few bottles of wine, maybe some time exploring each other's bodies. He'd like nothing more than to learn her body, know what gave her pleasure, what brought her to ecstasy. From top to bottom.

He scanned his boarding pass at the gate, and the flight attendant smiled. "Welcome aboard, Mr. Baron."

In the conference room, a dozen C-level and director-level folks sat around an oval table—some he'd met when he'd pitched his services a month prior. Hunter loved to see such a diverse group. It told him Zeo was forward-thinking and that almost always translated into success.

Hunter stood to address them. "At the thirty-thousand-foot level, Zeo has some incredible things going for it. Your financial backing is solid, your OS product-integration is excellent—" The R&D director nodded. "And most apps are rich in content." A few more heads nodded. "That said, that rich content means straddling a fine line between performance and battery life." He motioned with both hands, his arm akimbo.

The CEO, Phillip Brinley, lifted a brow. That may have been news to him.

The head of HR shifted in her chair. "We also struggle with finding talent. Local talent."

"I get it. You want to make sure you maintain one hundred percent onshore talent."

Her lips curved upward.

"Another challenge—getting noticed. It is still the number one struggle for mobile app developers. One thing you can do, aside from making a great product, is to mimic successful apps. I took a look at your competition, and here's what I've learned." Several folks leaned forward—hopefully they were impressed by Hunter's attention to detail, but this was precisely why firms hired him.

He pressed the light on the projector to illuminate the screen before them, then walked them step-by-step through his findings—some apps had recognizable designs and colors. He pointed out what users found interesting as well as confusing.

The meeting progressed for another thirty-five minutes, and from the nods and questions, Hunter knew everyone was onboard.

"We've covered a lot here today, and I'll be finalizing our plan of action soon. First, I have a list of questions for the team. Sort of a homework assignment." Chuckles were heard as Hunter passed out a single sheet to everyone, then returned to his place at the head of the table. "My initial task—sorta the shark closest to the boat—centers on the fact that ten percent of your success falls on the app itself, ninety percent falls on marketing." He looked at Chanise, the head of sales and marketing. "I'd like to meet with your team next week to review ways to optimize your strategies."

She met his gaze with eager eyes.

The meeting wrapped up and Hunter felt good overall. He knew he'd hit on their key points. The CEO even had some complimentary words, which Hunter suspected weren't easy to come by.

As the room cleared, Chanise approached him, a young woman in her upper thirties with long straight hair pulled back in a slick ponytail. "I appreciate the work you've done here, Hunter. You and your team put together an excellent presentation."

His team. He could chuckle every time he heard those words. His team was himself and Rebecca "Becca" Kim, an NYU grad who'd grown tired of the northern cold weather and moved back to Texas, to her parents' delight. He'd lucked out in finding her. Becca was like a super-smart girl-Friday who could answer his phone and book appointments, then a minute later read a client's financial statements to determine how much they were spending on radio advertising.

"Thank you," he replied.

"Maybe we can head to my office and schedule an exact time for you to meet with my team."

"Excellent." He followed her out of the conference room down the hall to a nicely appointed space with a desk, a round meeting table and chairs, and a view of downtown Dallas.

Chanise immediately walked behind her large glass-top desk and picked up the phone. "Virginia, do you have a moment?"

He eyed her curiously.

Chanise flipped her ponytail to the back. "Virginia is my right-hand man, so to speak."

"I heard that." The woman in question strode into the office. She wore a navy pantsuit, minimal makeup, and short brunette hair. Her handshake was strong and her smile sincere.

"Ginny, this is Hunter Baron, the consultant Phillip hired. He has some great ideas to help capitalize on our rapid growth. I'd like to see when you, Bradley, and Jon could meet with him and get the ball rolling." Chanise motioned to her conference table.

"Ginny" opened her phone and gave Hunter a few options for the following week. Chanise watched her and chatted, almost as if they were more friends than co-workers.

They talked for several more minutes, both women's gazes trained on him, focused, and seemingly hanging onto his every word.

Hunter often met with people whose company was in a state of transition—either high-growth or serious decline in sales. They'd been anxious for his help and guidance, but he'd rarely received such an eager reception. Chanise and Ginny had intuitive questions, were friendly, even joking at times. He felt positive about their ability to work with him and propel the company to the next level.

With the next steps solidified, he rose and shook hands.

"Great to meet you, Hunter," Ginny held his hand, making a half-step into his personal space. "Looking forward to next week.”

He made his way to the rental car and called Becca to touch base and see if he’d missed anything.

“Nothing too much going on, boss, just a call from Roland Pepper at Frisco Foods.” Roland was one of his meetings the next day while in town.

“Thanks, Becca. I’ll call him when I get back to the hotel. I’ll be here again next Wednesday. We can wait to book the flight tomorrow though. Wanna see if Frisco needs me as well.”

“Okay, boss.”

He disconnected the line and let his thoughts wander as he drove through Dallas traffic. Rachel popped into his mind, her smile and her vanilla scent filling his psyche. Maybe this was a good time to let her in on their date plans.

Rachel’s cell phone dinged from the corner of her desk. She had it set that way to minimize distraction while she worked. Her heart gave a little pitter-patter when she saw it was Hunter.

“Hello.”

“Hello, beautiful. How’s your day going?”

“Good. What are you up to? I’m surprised to hear from you.” She couldn’t keep the smile off her face.

“I’m sitting in traffic, heading back to the hotel, and you were on my mind.”

Holy cow! “Really? How sweet.”

"So about Friday..."

Crap! He's cancelling.

"You might want to wear jeans. And do you own any cowboy boots?"

She breathed a sigh of relief, then her eyebrows pulled together. *Jeans? Cowboy boots?* Maybe they were going to the rodeo. "I do have jeans and cowboy boots. Where are we going?"

"Uh-uh. It's a surprise. You'll find out. I'll pick you up at seven."

She grinned like a teenager.

"Hey, that's another call coming in. I'll see you Friday, Rachel. Can't wait."

"See you Friday." She sat and stared at nothing, the smile still plastered on her lips. She almost didn't care where they were going. It was great that Hunter was taking her out on a date.

Roger entered her cubicle. "Hey Rachel, would you update the Watson spreadsheet with these figures and send it to Karl in Accounting, please?" He handed her a paper with his handwriting scratched over it. He didn't leave immediately.

"Sure." She waited. "Is there something else?"

His head tilted. "You look particularly happy. Something good must have happened."

"I have a date Friday with Hunter."

Crap! She hated that she blurted out what she thought.

Most people practiced restraint and held it in. She didn't want to tell Roger right away about Hunter. There really wasn't much to tell anyway.

His lips curved at the corners. "Good for you. I had a good feeling about you two." He spun around and headed back to his office.

Oh gees! She lowered her forehead to her open palm. She might never hear the end of this.

Chapter Nine

HUNTER'S HAND RESTED at the base of Rachel's back, guiding her through the parking lot, and she loved it. It was funny how something seemingly so commonplace with him felt so incredibly special to her.

Muffled music emanated from the large building. The sign overhead read Rosco's.

This definitely isn't the rodeo.

They walked to the hostess stand. "Reservation for Baron."

Rachel's gaze traveled the space—a large restaurant with hardwood floors and lights made out of Mason jars hung over the wooden tables. There looked to be about two hundred people seated, and they still had room for more. Waitstaff dashed about with white aprons fastened over all-black uniforms. The hostess led them to a table where the music, although distant, seemed to get louder.

Despite the expanse of the place, it still had a welcoming

and cozy feel.

"I hope you like Tex-Mex," Hunter said with a grin. "They have some of the best around. The chefs always put a twist on it."

She nodded as she laid her coat over the empty chair, and before she could ask about the music, the waiter arrived. The man relayed the dinner specials and took their drink orders.

"I've been coming here for years. It may seem casual, but everything on the menu is excellent." Hunter's eyes twinkled in the dim light.

He looked so damn handsome in his crisp white button-down shirt, dark blue jeans, and black leather cowboy boots.

"Where's the music coming from?" It wasn't too loud to be distracting, but curiosity reigned.

He winked. "That's the surprise, for later."

Her heart kicked over. She hadn't dated much and missed all those wonderful "new" things: fresh conversation, first kisses, the intimacy. Being this close to Hunter, her mind took her to those places. From their dance together at the Gala, she'd wanted him, and wanted all those firsts.

The food arrived and the conversation flowed effortlessly. They shared many similar interests, like music, movies, books, even vacation spots. Not that she got to vacation much, but she had a list. A sorta bucket list for travel.

Then the topic of the Gala came up. He leaned closer.

"You dance very well."

Warmth crept into her cheeks as she thought of how he'd held her. "I took dance lessons when I was little—tap, jazz, and ballet. I thoroughly enjoyed it but couldn't keep up with everything going on at the time, so it was the thing that had to go."

"So, what did you do instead?" He forked his grilled steak and popped it into his mouth.

"Cheerleading. Turns out being good at dance makes you an excellent candidate for cheerleading."

He grinned at her. "So do you have any cheerleaders or dancers in the house now?"

Hunter was asking about her kids, and the thought touched her. She shook her head as she sipped on her white wine. "A flutist and a football player."

"Excellent."

"Yup. My daughter, Violet, is eleven and plays flute. My son, Ethan, plays flag football. I'm holding off putting him in pads as long as I can."

Hunter gave her a knowing nod. "I played football in high school, and my mother was always worried about injuries." He drank from his mug of beer. "I take it they get to see their father regularly."

"Mm-hm. Every other weekend, alternating holidays, and two weeks during the summer." She set her fork down because this was her opportunity to address her divorce so there was nothing left hidden. "He's a good dad, but was a lousy husband. He has a very controlling demeanor, and whenever I'd push back, it would always turn into an argument. Divorce seemed to be the only answer, for the sake of the kids too."

Hunter hadn't specifically asked about her divorce but showed no sign that her divulging bothered him. He nodded with understanding.

She knew the opportunity was ripe for asking about his past loves. "So, enough about me. How 'bout you? Ever been married or at least engaged?"

He glanced down before meeting her gaze. "I was married once. It's in the past. If it's all right with you, I'd rather not talk about it."

She stared for a moment and swallowed hard. "Okay." She hadn't expected that response. But what could she say? Hunter seemed so open and gregarious. *I guess not about everything.*

He quickly refilled her wine glass. "Care to have dessert?"

She sighed. Her mind still raced, and she wondered if he'd had a bad divorce like hers. "No, thanks."

He winked. "Probably a good idea. We don't want to be too full for the rest of the evening."

Rachel was simply enchanting. Dinner was tops, with the exception of her question about being married.

Damn! He should have been prepared for that. Jessica

was dead and wouldn't be coming back. There was nothing to discuss. But he could have handled it better.

They had to have a flawless evening. He wanted to show Rachel a good time. And for some inexplicable reason, he needed to show her he could be a gentleman. She'd probably had her fair share of guys setting their sights on one thing. It would be hard not to want that from such a beautiful woman. As much as Hunter would love to please her in that way, he would wait. At least one night, he could wait.

After pushing through a large wooden swinging door, the confusion on Rachel's face began to fade. He guided her down the short wide hallway to the dance hall.

Her eyes rounded.

"Everything make sense now?"

"We're gonna country dance?"

"Yes, ma'am." He gave his best Texas twang.

She continued to study the area that was as big as the front restaurant, but this was strictly for dancing and drinking. In the center was a dance floor shaped like a rectangle with rounded corners where couples danced in a circuit to a Garth Brooks song. The space surrounding the dance floor held onlookers and one of the largest bars Hunter had ever seen.

She stretched up to say in his ear, "I don't know how to country dance."

He figured there was a chance of that, but that wasn't about to stop them. "No problem. I'll teach you." Glancing at her purse and coat, he said, "How about we drop those off at the coat check?"

Hand-in-hand, he led her to the coat check attendant and slipped her jacket off her arm. Rachel wore straight blue jeans that hugged her ass to perfection, a thin-knit pink sweater, brown cowboy boots, a silver necklace at the base of her throat and matching dangly earrings. She looked so incredible that he could devour her from top to bottom.

They walked to the railing that outlined the entire dance floor so they could get a good view of the dancers moving counterclockwise. He quickly found a couple with great technique to point out for her.

Rachel's jaw dropped. "Hunter, I don't know about this."

Hunter followed her line of sight. A couple closer to the inside of the floor moved effortlessly, and the woman spun around several times. They'd clearly been dancing together for a long time.

"It's okay. We don't have to do anything too advanced. Look at those two." He gestured to a couple close to the perimeter. "Watch their steps. Slow, slow, quick, quick." The speed of his speech matched the words he said and matched the beat of the music.

"What?" She glanced up at him.

"That's how the steps are best described: one *slow* step for two beats, and a quick step is one step for one beat."

They observed the couple move in a walking pattern

around the dance floor.

"Oh, I see it. Slow, slow, quick, quick."

"Just like you're walking."

She grinned. "Except I don't walk backwards."

He smiled back. "I won't let you run into anyone."

They watched through the rest of the song. Then, it was time to try. The next song had a simple beat that would be great for learning to Two Step.

"Ready?"

Rachel visibly swallowed and scrunched her nose. Stinkin' adorable. "I guess so," she strung out the words.

"C'mon." He clasped her hand and led her to a break in the railing to enter the dance floor. He placed his hands on her—one on her shoulder, one on her waist—with distance between them to comfortably move. "Okay, I'm gonna start with my left leg, you're gonna start with your right."

She nodded.

"Hear the beat. Slow, slow, quick, quick," he said the words to the beat.

They started moving and she peered down at their feet. "It's okay, Rachel. Look at me. Slow, slow, quick, quick." They danced, making one complete lap around the dance floor. "That's right. See how the sand helps you to almost slide across the floor?"

She nodded.

"You got it. You're a natural." Her graceful moves took his mind back to the Gala weeks ago.

Rachel whispered. "Slow, slow, quick, quick."

He grinned. "Soon, you'll be able to talk to me without it throwing off your steps. We've gone around twice so far."

Her eyes twinkled. "I like it."

He somehow knew she would.

Moving on to the next song, they didn't miss a beat. He felt confident they could try and turn. "Ready for the next part?"

Her jaw gaped. "Uh, I think so."

"We're going to add in a turn. You'll let go of my shoulder and turn on the quick-steps."

She swallowed. "Okay, just let me know when."

"I'll count one, two, and three. You go after the two."

He lifted her right arm, giving her nudge. Her turn was perfect. She caught on quickly.

"Great. Let's do a few more, then get a drink."

They danced for the rest of the song, her footsteps so certain it was like she glided on air. Her years of formal dance training made her a natural. A sheen coated her upper lip.

He held her hand as the song ended, and the DJ called for a line dance. Perfect timing for them to get something refreshing.

He handed her a cold beer as she leaned against the railing surrounding the dance floor.

"Thanks." Rachel took a swig. "You don't strike me as a cowboy," she said over the music.

He chuckled. "I'm not. The Two Step is the most popular

couples' dance in the nation. I sorta like it." Hunter lifted a shoulder. He wouldn't get into details about how he and Jessica could spend hours country dancing.

"I like it too. I'm so glad you brought me here."

After the line dance, the DJ called for a slow couples' dance. "Ready to head back out there?"

She nodded and held his hand as he led her to a spot on the floor. With the lights turned down, the feeling was cozy and romantic. This time, he pulled her closer into him, their legs woven between each other as they slowly made their way around.

"You're a natural, Rachel," he said in a voice just above a whisper.

Her body molded to his, just as it had when they'd danced at the Gala.

"You're a good dancer too. You make it easy to follow you." Her gaze locked with his for several beats, and he didn't resist the temptation. He lowered his lips to hers in a gentle kiss. A kiss that turned more passionate as he let go of her right hand and wrapped his arm around her waist, drawing closer.

Her hand cupped his neck, and she kissed him, humming her delight.

He wanted her. For all that was good, he wanted her. Naked, on his bed, open to receive all he had to give her.

He broke the kiss, acutely aware they were in a public place. Not to mention he desperately wanted to exercise more control, more restraint. He couldn't say why he lost his head so easily around Rachel, but dammit, he had to maintain some level of control. She was different than the other friends with benefits he'd had. He and Rachel weren't necessarily going to jump into bed immediately.

Soon, he reassured himself. "Do you have the kids tomorrow night?"

"Um, no, but I have a commitment already. My best friend arranged a birthday dinner for me."

His eyes rounded. "Oh, happy birthday. Wow, I didn't know."

She gave a shy smile. "How could you?"

Damn! He had to see her before his next business trip. "Then how about Sunday?"

"I get the kids back at four o'clock on Sunday."

Fuck a duck! "Okay, we'll figure out something," he said, hoping the words would become reality.

Chapter Ten

THE ITALIAN RESTAURANT easily accommodated their party of twelve for Rachel's birthday celebration. Appetizers were served, and the drinks flowed. It was good to connect with her friends again, some she hadn't seen since before the divorce.

Secretly, she'd been dreading the night, preferring a quiet dinner with just a few friends. Rachel was getting older and while overall things were going great, something felt a bit off-track, and she was running out of time to correct course. But now with Hunter in her life, even momentarily, things seemed better all around. Hunter might not be a true partner, but she was lonely for companionship, and for *that* he fit the bill.

Just before the entrées arrived, her phone flashed a text from Hunter.

I hope you have a great night. I have a present for you. Can you do brunch in the morning?

Her tummy did a little flip.

TY. Yes, that sounds great.

Her date with Hunter the prior night had been exceptional—the dinner, the dancing, all of it. He'd held her close again for several dances that made her heart race. His kisses and caresses sent shivers to her core. But when he'd taken her home and kissed her goodnight, she was dumbfounded. She was certain he'd accept her invitation to come in. Don't all men want sex? With all they'd already done, weren't they to that point?

She'd scolded herself for her disappointment. Her attachment to Hunter was clearly growing but she couldn't handle any more disappointment from a man.

Where was that *laissez-faire* attitude she was supposed to implement?

"So, have you told her where we're going next?" Monique's voice yanked her from her thoughts, directing the question to Lexi.

Lexi grinned and shook her head. "I thought we'd just show up."

A few of her friends chuckled, some nodded, and Monique said, "I think that's a great idea."

Rachel didn't like the sound of that. "So, I don't get a vote in any of this?"

Alexis didn't miss a beat. "Nope. Now, open your

presents so we can be there by nine."

Rachel scooped up the last bite of tiramisu and pushed her plate away. One by one she opened her presents: a silk scarf, scented candles, a plush throw, so many wonderful things, she felt special. Polly and Lexi were the most audacious in the group, so she shouldn't have been surprised that they'd bought her lingerie.

"It will be good when you get out there to put your best sexy-self forward." Polly winked.

Rachel could only smile. Her friends beamed, and after the checks were paid, they all piled into cabs and headed somewhere she had no clue.

After several minutes, the caravan came to a stop. Rachel gasped.

In bold lettering above an iron door the words *Le Nu Hommes* singed her eyeballs. She knew from her French classes, it read "the naked men".

"Ohmigod," she breathed out, then threw a look at Lexi. Her eyes narrowed. "A strip club?!"

Her friends in the car grinned. Lexi only shrugged a shoulder. "Think Magic Mike. It'll be great." Her eyebrows waggled.

Rachel hadn't been to a strip club since her twenties, back when she was single.

Oh Lordy, she thought. She needed to remember that tonight was about having fun and laughing with friends.

The ladies piled out of the cab and headed toward the

velvet-roped entrance. Lexi went to the front of the line and flashed a smile at the tall, burly doorman.

"Evening, ladies."

"Evening. We're celebrating our friend's birthday. We have a reservation. It would be under Johnson." Enunciating her last name and drawing it out, Lexi glanced at the clipboard he held.

Polly and Tracey giggled at the play on words.

Really, Rachel had good friends, mature and level-headed. But nights like this, they let it all hang out, not bothering with perfect manners. Reverting back to teenage behavior came naturally.

The ladies took their seats at a large, leather-covered, semi-circle booth on a dais with a perfect view of the stage. Within minutes, the wait staff had set down water glasses and champagne flutes with a bottle on ice.

"Shall I pop your cork, ladies?" the shirtless waiter asked with a wink, pouring a few ounces in everyone's glass.

More giggling.

"Enjoy the show." He walked off giving everyone a nice view of his taut derriere.

"Oh, we will." Lexi raised her glass for a toast. "To our girl, Rachel. May this mark a new beginning. To new beginnings."

The girls chimed in, "To new beginnings."

With only a minute or two to spare, the lights dimmed, and the show started. The announcer introduced the dancers and the music began. The audience screamed and applauded as six men took the stage to do their routine. Ties came off, followed by shirts, a few hats, until the *pièce de résistance*: their pants flew off. The crowd went wild. Rachel chuckled as she clapped, cheering on the muscular men stripped down to thongs.

A few more shows followed that were a variety of male dancers in different costumes gyrating to loud songs with a strong beat.

Alexis ordered another bottle of champagne after the first one went so quickly.

The MC made an announcement of Rachel's birthday and two shirtless, six-foot hunks in red bowties and black pants approached their table. A fun I'll-love-you-all-night song came on and the girls hooted and hollered as the men lured her to the stage.

"Oh, shit," she breathed out. She should have been prepared for Lexi arranging something completely unexpected.

Placed on a simple wooden chair in the center of the stage, the men took turns giving her lap dances, tipping her back to plant playful kisses on her neck. They straddled her and caressed her arms and legs. Within a few beats the playfulness ended.

A small jolt of panic flew through her as she was lifted by one man, her legs kicking overhead until she was basically straight above him upside down.

"Eee." She tried to stifle her surprise. It all happened so fast. Thank God, she'd decided on her new slacks last minute.

He set her down easily, grinning, as he knew exactly what he was doing.

The second dancer grabbed both her wrists, and before she could protest, he had slipped a wide, red satin ribbon around them.

Her heart hammered against her ribcage.

The first dancer must have read her panic because quickly he lifted her, letting her straddle his waist, and whispered in her ear, "Relax. We won't hurt you, I promise. We want to keep our license." He leaned back and grinned, his eyes twinkling.

She inhaled, allowing herself to go with the theme of sexy fun.

He backed her to a chrome pole set in the middle of the stage and, carefully holding her body against his, let her slide down to her feet.

Dancer Number Two worked her arms high, tying her to the pole in five seconds flat, positioned with a side view to the crowd. Her table went wild, cheering and applauding.

The men continued their dance and gyrations, mostly it seemed for the benefit of the audience, and she was just fine with that.

Man Number One came up behind her, roaming his hands over her stomach, ass, and hips. He whispered in her ear, "You smell incredible. We're going to have a little more fun with you. Okay?"

She hesitantly nodded.

Soon, both men's hands roamed her clothed body, down her thighs and up her stomach, under her sweater. Fingers caressed from behind, shifting her legs farther apart.

Man Number One went down on his knees before her, caressing her thighs over her black slacks, skating a thumb along the inside. On the last upward motion, he lifted her sweater, revealing her stomach.

Rachel's breath hitched.

He placed several small kisses on her skin.

The audience went crazy.

He gave her a reassuring smile as his hands roamed her torso, inching to just below her bra.

Oh gees! She quickly searched her memory. *If he pulls up my sweater, what bra am I wearing?*

Suddenly, the man behind her stroked his hands up the outside of her thighs, feeling his way to her pants' button. He unbuttoned it and slightly tugged the fabric apart.

Her pulse raced. This was both exhilarating and scary. She licked her lips.

Her eyes found Lexi, who sent her an exuberant smile and a wink. She probably knew exactly what they were going to do to her.

More dancing with the men touching her. Hands glossed over her mons and breasts, and her heart kicked over. She tried not to flinch at the surprising exhilarating movements.

Man Number One stood close before her, kissing her neck, moving his hips to mimic humping her. "Fuck, birthday girl, do you have any idea how hot you look right now?"

She moaned. It wasn't planned. None of this was. She was held captive, and it didn't matter that there were a hundred women watching. Her body reacted in a purely physical way. Hunter flashed in her head, and she couldn't help but wish those hands, those kisses, were his.

The dancer's last little brush connected with her sex, and she realized he was semi-hard. The dancer went lower. He played with her sweater hem, lifting it and bringing it back down, teasing the audience, like there was about to be a big reveal.

Oh, God. They wouldn't, would they?

Oh no, that's not what they had in mind. Man Number One lifted her sweater just enough to allow his head to fit underneath. Then quicker than a blink of eye, reached his hands under, yanked her bra cups down and laved at her nipples.

Her head fell back as sensation ricocheted throughout her body.

The crowd went insane, louder than the times before. She couldn't look at them. Her eyelids fell closed as his ministrations superseded any other sensory input.

He laved and sucked for she didn't know how long. Hunter popped in her head again, and she moaned.

Oh hell!

The glorious torture only lasted another few seconds. The man was good; he'd done this a time or two, maybe on this stage, maybe not.

He popped his head out from under her sweater, pulling it down, not bothering to put her bra back in place. Both men kissed her neck, and as Man Number Two untied her, Man Number One smiled and whispered in her ear, "I bet you're an incredible fuck."

The song ended.

Like some sex princess descending from her altar, they escorted her down the steps and back to her table. The MC rambled on about something Rachel couldn't even hear. Her head was spinning. Did that really just happen?

The grins on her girls' faces told her it had, that she hadn't just imagined it.

"Holy shit," Lexi leaned in. "Did he do what we think he did?"

She pulled her lips between her teeth and lifted her hands to discreetly pop her breasts back in their cups.

"Holy shit." Lexi repeated herself, her jaw gaping in utter amazement.

Rachel's mouth was parched but she managed to say, "I need a drink."

Polly quickly refilled her glass from the bottle sitting in the ice bucket.

Rachel sat there, processing and gulping her

champagne, slickness where she sat. This was definitely a night she would not soon forget.

Maybe turning forty ain't so bad?

The performance on the stage, while entertaining, did not detract from the ache that resided at the apex of her thighs. Nor did it distract her mind from thinking about her current infatuation, Hunter.

She wanted to text him. God help her, she wanted to see if he was still awake.

Shit! What did she really have to lose? She glanced at the time. Eleven o'clock.

Her fingers flew over the screen.

Hi! Are you up?

Goodness, she was a juvenile. What was she thinking? Hell, he could have been with someone, a woman. The thought clenched her stomach.

His reply vibrated her phone.

Yes. What's up? Everything ok?

How should she reply? She had to see him. Tonight.

Can you come pick me up?

That was all she could type. Her heart raced. This was like sexting, or something. Gees! She was crazy.

Yes. Where are you?

She exhaled. Typing out the name of the place, Lexi caught her eye. She glanced up.

"Texting Mr. Tall, Dark, and Handsome?"

Rachel bit the inside of her cheek. "Yes. Are you mad?"

Lexi chuckled. "Not at all. It's your birthday. Time for your birthday boink."

Rachel felt her face get hot.

"Don't worry about a thing here. We'll take care of it. Go be with your man."

Chapter Eleven

THERE WAS SOMETHING so incredibly pleasing and yet mocking in pulling up in front of this…nightclub to pick up the vivacious Rachel. When Hunter had gotten her text, he had no idea if something bad happened or something good.

Rachel stood outside with a friend, then strode to the side of his car. Her eyes sparkled and her cheeks were rosy, likely nothing to do with the coldness outside. He lowered the passenger-side window.

"Hi, handsome."

Why hearing her call him that made him beam inside he couldn't say. "Hi, beautiful."

"This is Alexis." She motioned to the woman beside her.

A smiley brunette with model-perfect red lips and a similar pink flush on her cheeks leaned into the car window, stretching her hand. "Nice to meet you, Hunter. Heard good things about you. Take care of our birthday girl, okay?"

"You bet I will."

Rachel hugged her friend and climbed into his sedan. She looked so fucking gorgeous in her snug black pants and jacket with a purple sweater showing a hint of cleavage. He wanted to pull her into him so he could feast on her precious mouth.

They drove away from the club and headed toward the freeway. "Did you have fun tonight?"

She glanced his way and glowed. "I did. It's been a long time since Lexi pulled together a party like that."

"Like a year?"

She laughed out loud, maybe more boisterous than her usual laugh. Yup, Rachel was a bit tipsy.

"Where are we going?" she asked after a minute of driving.

"I'm taking you home."

The car fell silent, and Rachel stared out the front windshield. "Oh."

His eyebrows pulled together. "Do you not want to go home?"

She faced him, the tip of her tongue darting out to wet her lips. "No. Take me to your place."

Fuck! What was she asking? "You want to go to my place?"

She nodded and leaned closer. "I want to go to your place. I want to roll around naked. I want you to make me come."

His dick came to life. She'd been drinking—at a strip club no less—but how much? He had a fine line to walk. If she was horny, that was one thing. If she was drunk, he'd bow out. "Rachel, I think it would be best if I took you home. It's late."

She paused then swung the seatbelt off her shoulder, resting a hand on his thigh. "I want you to fuck me, Hunter. I want you to make me scream." Then her hand slid over his erection. "I'm not too drunk to know just what I'm asking for."

Holy fuck! He glanced once more at her, seeing the sincerity and determination in her eyes. Pulling against the steering wheel, he hooked his first left to head the car toward his apartment.

Fuck if he didn't want to give her exactly what she needed. He wouldn't stop until she was satisfied. He lifted her hand, kissing the back. "I'd be happy to."

She grinned and returned to her seat for the short ride to his place.

They exited his car. He offered his hand, lacing his fingers between hers. The night air was cool, but inside his blood boiled. He couldn't wait to get this gorgeous woman completely naked, soaking in every ounce of her.

He held open the door for Rachel to walk through and locked it behind him.

She strode to his sofa and dropped her bag and her coat.

Her pupils dilated, her irises deep blue.

He moved close enough to feel her breasts scrape his chest as she stared up at him.

"Rachel, are you sure about this? Are you sure you want me to... to be with you?"

Her mouth parted as she nodded.

He didn't waste another minute. He grabbed her cheeks and lay claim to her plump pink lips. His tongue dove deep, and she whimpered. The need for one another fueled each other's desire.

He broke the kiss long enough to toss her sweater aside and tug off her sexy pants.

The sight of her in his dimly lit apartment was enough to take his breath away. His dick ached for her. He pulled her close once again, clutching the back of her neck for their lips to lock together while his free hand released the clasp of her bra, dropping it to the floor.

He leaned down to claim her pointed nipples, kneading her breasts as she clung to his shoulders and panted out his name.

First things first. He steered her a few feet to his large dining table. He whipped off his shirt to lay it before her then pushed her to bend forward onto the table.

Lust coursed through his veins like he was a possessed man. He couldn't wait to be inside her, hear her scream his name, make her come over and over.

She lay before him in nothing but a scrap of underwear,

her round ass beckoning him.

He dropped to his knees, and the scent of her permeated his core. "Fuck, you smell good," he breathed out.

With no ceremony, he ripped her thong in two, pushed against her thighs, and ravaged her soaking pussy.

"Hunter!"

He thrust his tongue into her cleft, forcing a moan from her. Over and over his tongue swirled against her engorged clit.

Her moans grew louder.

He retrieved a rubber from his back pocket. With two fingers, he pushed into her warm wet channel as his thumb spun over her hot button.

He rose, opening his jeans enough to pull out his dick to sheath himself.

Her precious little clit started to twitch.

He leaned over her. "That's right, my sexy woman. Come on my fingers."

And she did just that, pulling on his fingers and screaming out his name. When she'd nearly come down, he dove into her, and not a moment too soon. He didn't know if he could wait any longer.

"Hunter," she screamed again as she pushed back against him, building a rhythm together.

He released all his pent-up lust, raining praises and kisses over her back. Finally, he went lax over her, panting fiercely, hoping like hell he hadn't hurt her.

"Are you okay?"

She opened her glassy blue eyes to meet his gaze. "Yes. Ohmigosh, yes."

He smiled. He didn't want to leave her, but he had too. He'd come so hard and so long, the condom could have blown. He kissed her shoulder one last time. "I'll be right back."

He high-tailed it to his guest bathroom and disposed of the condom, then quickly wetted a washcloth to bring to her.

He returned to find her just as he'd left her, stark naked, legs spread, lying on his table. It was a sight he would never forget. His dick surged.

Carefully, he wiped her pussy and helped her to stand. He kissed her gently, wanting more. Wanting to show her he knew how to be a gentleman, and not just some sex-starved maniac.

Her hands skated up his arms to his chest. His firm, muscular chest. Rachel had to see him. She pulled back and wandered with her hands and her eyes. From his broad shoulders to his chest to his abs. His jeans and underwear where partially back in place.

Did that mean they were done?

She didn't want to be done.

Her hands moved over his length, feeling him recharge.

God, she loved that he was hard. Hard for her. She glanced up to see any sign of apprehension. There was none.

She slid her hands along his waistband, dipping her fingertips inside. Peeling away the fabric, she lowered herself to her knees. Meeting his eyes as she closed her lips over his head was perfect.

His eyelids fluttered and his hips flexed slightly. He placed his hands on her shoulders as she worked his length with her mouth.

"Rachel," he breathed out.

She licked the underneath, then swallowed him, letting him bump into her throat. Her mouth and hand worked him, stroking on the way down, sucking on the way up.

"Fuck, baby." His hands gripped her hair at the back of her head.

She knew he was close, and she was ready.

His cock spasmed once, twice, and he shot his load into her.

She took down every last drop, relishing the salty-sweet taste from a release she'd created.

Panting for air, he rested a hand on the table.

She rose, a smile on her face at how she'd affected him.

He hooked an arm around her waist and pulled her into him, crashing his lips to hers. His tongue dove deep, tangling with hers, telling her he wanted nothing else in the world just then except for her.

He broke the kiss, hovering close to her face. "Please come to my bed. Spend the night with me. I'll make us breakfast in the morning." His eyes pleaded with her.

There was only one good answer. "Yes."

Chapter Twelve

RACHEL STIRRED. THE smell of bacon lingered in the air. It only took a split-second to recognize where she was, and who she'd been with.

Mmm.

The most delicious, exhilarating, and satisfying night she'd had in a long time. Three times. Three times they'd made love last night. So crazy good!

Glancing to the right, she saw Hunter's side of the bed lay empty.

Her actions from the night before flashed into her head, reminding her of all the insanity at the club, then her subsequent booty call.

No, it wasn't a booty call.

Yes, it sure was. Women can make booty calls too.

She groaned inwardly.

Gees! What he must think.

Time to face the music. She slipped out from under the

covers and scowled not seeing her panties. *Oh, that's right, he ripped them.* She grabbed his button-down shirt draped over the chair and headed to the bathroom.

After a few short minutes, she strode into the kitchen to see Hunter working at the cooktop, flipping the bacon, dressed in long pajama bottoms and a T-shirt.

"Morning."

He glanced up, the corners of his lips curved. "Morning."

She reached for a mug to fill with coffee. *Oh shit, he didn't buy the cheap stuff.*

He flipped off the burner and set down the tongs, strolling closer to her. "I was just thinking about you." His voice dipped, running over her like warm, rich caramel.

"You were?" Her breath hitched as he moved behind her, pressing against her backside.

Oh wow! He was hard.

"Uh-huh. And I can't tell you how happy I am that you called me last night."

Heat saturated her cheeks. "I'm sorry about that."

He pushed her hair aside and pulled against his shirt collar to give him access to her neck. "No. You don't get to be sorry. That was a phenomenal night. One I'd like to live over and over... starting right now." His kisses were bone-melting, leaving a hot trail in their wake.

His hands caressed her thighs up to her ass under the shirt—kneading, stroking, making her crave more.

"I love seeing you in my shirt." He reached up to caress her breasts and toy with her nipples. "I especially love the no-panties."

"I couldn't... find them. Besides, someone ripped them," she challenged.

"I'll make it up to you." Expert hands roamed her body.

She swallowed, and her muscles clenched deep inside. Her breathing escalated.

He kicked her feet wider as he pressed her back, folding her over the counter. "Besides, they'd only get in the way." A finger slid right up the middle of her liquid heat.

"Oh God," she breathed out.

His finger worked her clit with his right hand as his left lifted the shirt out of the way, exposing her naked backside to him.

It didn't matter. Her need was too great. He'd built her to an incredible lather and she needed release. She would beg if she had to.

He caressed her needy clit while laying kisses over her back, occasionally licking and nipping at her skin.

Then the sound of a crinkled wrapper came from behind her. A condom.

Yes!

"Do you want that, sweetheart? Do you want me to take you from behind, make you come, standing here in my kitchen?"

"Yes. Yes, Hunter, please."

Without any hesitation, he dove his thick cock into her. Oh, sweet lord.

"Baby, you feel incredible." With a slight pull, he gave her more distance from the countertop, enough to reach her clit.

"Hunter."

His ministrations were incredible. She never knew her body was capable of such pleasure. "Please," she begged, not knowing for what reason. "Please."

With several more thrusts, her orgasm exploded, shattering her into a million tiny, sparkling pieces. Shortly after, he released as well, growling out her name, panting at her neck.

He held her as he kissed her hair, her neck, and her shoulder. "So perfect."

"Mmmhmm." It was. She glowed from the inside.

He reached for a towel, blotting her as he slipped out. He pitched the condom and put himself back together, catching her stare.

She sucked in her lower lip, and he smiled. Then she lifted her coffee for a sip. Back to the regularly scheduled programming.

"How do you like your eggs?" he asked as he lifted the bacon out of the fry pan.

She bit back a grin. "Scrambled is great."

Hunter retrieved plates out of the cabinet, and she took them to set the table. They worked side-by-side, like they'd done it a thousand times.

Rachel sat with him to enjoy their first breakfast together at his table. She was starving. Sex definitely worked up an appetite.

When they were done, he wiped his mouth and leaned his elbows on the table. "Rachel, I have a birthday present for you."

She sat up taller and grinned. He was good at dates and surprises.

"I need to plan a business trip," he started, "to San Francisco." He pulled an envelope from the empty chair beside him and slid it to her. "I was hoping you could join me."

She looked down and opened the envelope to see a printed itinerary in two weeks, first class plane tickets, no less.

"If I did my math right, you won't have your kids that weekend. I thought we could spend one night in Napa." His eyes shone with anticipation. "You mentioned you love wine."

His gift touched her. Never had she ever received such a wonderful gift from a man. "I've never been to San Francisco or Napa."

"Then, you'll come?"

He was right, she didn't have the kids that weekend. The departure flight meant she'd have to leave work a little early, but Roger wouldn't have an issue with that. Getting Richie to pick up the kids from school would be a little challenge, but she'd cross that bridge later.

She glanced up from the sheet to see the relaxed, sanguine face she'd come to enjoy more and more. Hope brimmed.

She couldn't say why she was hesitant, maybe it was simply the fear of falling for him. Of putting herself out there, being vulnerable, and risking getting burned.

You know you want this.

Before she could talk herself out of it, she replied, "Yes. I'd love to go with you."

He leaned closer to her and grasped her chin, kissing her. The first kiss was chaste and direct, almost a thank you. The second, he tilted his head and dove deeply, sending a warm tingling throughout her body.

How he did this to her every time, she had no idea. But she liked it. Maybe too much.

"Excellent." Hunter smiled at her. "You have a few hours before you have to be back, right?" He should take her home but somehow he couldn't let her go.

"Yes."

"I need to do a little shopping, a few things I want to pick up for the condo. Would you care to come with me?"

She averted her gaze and nibbled on her bottom lip.

"What is it, Rachel?"

"I don't have panties to wear."

A smile blossomed inside. "That's okay, we can make

that our first stop."

Her cheeks colored rosy as she nodded.

"Great. You help yourself to the shower. I'll clean up here."

They'd both showered and dressed quickly. Hunter had planned to go shopping that day for some basics—lightbulbs, place mats, batteries—then pack because his flight out to Phoenix was first thing in the morning. Having her tag along was the cherry on top.

Truth be told, if he hadn't cleaned the kitchen, he would have joined her in the shower and taken her again. Just kissing her had made him hard, and he was damn thankful the table obstructed her view. But here they were in some lingerie store, and all he could fucking think about was Rachel in those lacy, satiny garments.

Fuck!

He discreetly adjusted himself as he leaned in to whisper in her ear, "Rachel, I want to buy you a few things for our trip. Will you let me do that?"

She looked up him; her almost-innocence coming to the realization of the depth of his request. "Okay," she replied timidly.

He asked her size and pulled a few things off the racks, keeping his desire to buy everything in check. He handed her the garments, wishing he could see them on her. "Please try them all on. I want to buy whatever fits."

She nodded and escaped to the dressing rooms.

If he thought he could get away with it, he'd sneak in there with her. *Hell yeah.* And not just for the fashion show.

Several minutes later, his erection still in place, she came out with two stacks—one big, one small. She handed him the bigger one, and a tag from the panties that she'd kept on.

"These all fit."

He smiled. "Excellent. I'll be right back."

He made a beeline for the checkout counter and of course, bought the additional delicate laundry soap and a lingerie travel bag that the salesclerk recommended. He was on such a damn high, he'd buy Rachel anything.

Rachel waited by the door for him. Stepping outside, she pushed onto her toes to kiss him. "Thank you. You didn't have to do that."

He looped an arm around her waist, kissing her more deeply. "I know," he whispered over her lips. "I wanted to."

He knew he was deliberately staying in the moment with Rachel. Past friends with benefits wouldn't linger—either he would leave or she would. They certainly wouldn't go shopping. In this case, the feelings of guilt would have to be reconciled later.

Chapter Thirteen

HUNTER PARKED HIS car in front of Rachel's house as she'd directed. A black pickup truck sat in her driveway. By the frown on her face, it was not *her* truck.

He might have made a critical error in taking Rachel shopping, and consequentially bringing her home at three-fifteen in the afternoon. She'd said the kids would be back at four.

"Um, you don't have to walk me in." A nervous nibble of her lip had him guessing what to do next.

The sadistic side of him wanted to meet this ex. No, *had* to meet this ex. So many questions ran through his head, the greatest of which—why does he have access to *her* house? Hunter knew that this man elicited strong emotions from Rachel that were less than positive. "If it's alright with you, I'd prefer to walk you in. A gentleman doesn't drop a lady at the curb, and if your children are in there, they need to see that firsthand."

The corner of her lip raised, and her back seemed to straighten. "Okay. Just so you know, my ex, Richie, is here."

He nodded once.

Carrying her shopping bag, he followed her into the house, and a spring pink and green wreath bobbled against the door.

"Mom!" A bubbly blonde girl ran up to Rachel and wrapped her arms around Rachel's waist.

"Hi, pumpkin."

"Mom, I got it! I got picked to go to Austin for Battle of the Bands." Her cherub cheeks glowed as she beamed up at her mother.

"Oh baby, that's great. I knew you would get it." Rachel kissed the top of her head and squeezed her tight.

A young boy with brown hair and Rachel's same blue eyes approached. "Hey, Mom."

"Hey, Ethan. Kids, this is Mr. Hunter. Hunter, this is Violet and Ethan."

"Hi." Two sets of eyes looked up at him. "Violet, Ethan. Nice to meet you."

Violet grabbed her hand. "C'mon, Mom. We're making a cake."

Rachel visibly swallowed as she followed the kids into the kitchen.

A man, probably an inch or two shorter than Hunter, poured chocolate liquid from a big glass bowl into a metal cake pan. He looked up, glancing from Rachel to him and back to Rachel.

"Richie," Rachel said. "What's going on?"

"We arrived early and decided to bake a cake while we waited for you to... return." The edge in his voice was just subtle enough for the kids to miss, but not the adults. The man slid the cake into the oven.

"Richie, this is Hunter."

Hunter happily reached his hand to the man, damn-near forcing him to shake it. The maneuver wasn't meant to intimidate as much as show him he wouldn't be intimidated.

The smile didn't reach Richie's eyes, as to be expected. Instead his gaze darted back to Rachel. "Well, I think you've got it from here," he muttered.

Rachel's shoulders lowered slightly. "Okay, thanks for taking them."

Hunter mentally scratched his head. Why was she thanking him? Wasn't this part of his obligation as their father?

Richie kissed and hugged his children goodbye. Murmured a goodbye to Rachel and him as he headed to the front door, quickly closing it behind him.

She exhaled. It wasn't loud but Hunter heard it.

Okay, this man seemed to wield some kind of power over Rachel. He'd likely want to chat with her about this later, try to understand who he was to her, in her life, and what he wanted.

"So, did you go to my mom's birthday dinner?" Violet

hopped on the barstool.

"No, not this time," he replied to the curious creature.

"Are you a new friend? I don't recognize you." Ethan crossed his arms.

"Ethan," Rachel scolded.

"It's okay," he told her. "I *am* a new friend. That's probably why we've never met before."

"What do you do?" Violet asked.

"I own my own company. I consult with other companies that are growing fast or sometimes not growing enough."

Ethan's eyebrows lifted. "Like Apple?"

He grinned. Rachel had some smart kids. "Something like that, except Apple doesn't really need my help. They're handling things just fine, don't ya think?"

"I suppose."

Hunter seemed to have gained a little credibility with Ethan, who no doubt might be in business for himself someday.

"How good are you at dividing fractions?" Violet asked with the same innocence he'd seen in Rachel's eyes.

"Um, sweetie, I'll help you. Mr. Hunter needs to get going. Why don't you both get your homework and meet me in the kitchen? You can get some work done before dinner."

The kids high-tailed upstairs.

She turned to meet his gaze, a furrow in her brow. "I'm sorry about my ex."

"Your kids are awesome."

Her jaw closed, and her eyes softened. "Thank you."

"I'm gonna head out." He clasped her hand and walked them toward the front door. "I have a trip, but I'll call you when I return." A quick glance showed no little peering eyes on them. He cupped her jaw and leaned down, gliding his lips over hers.

Her hands slid up his arms, snaking around his neck. She opened for him.

He dove deep into her exquisite mouth, savoring it for as long as possible until he could taste her again.

"I had an amazing weekend." He pecked her lips one last time before he pulled the door open.

"Me too," she replied with a grin.

He sent her a wink before closing his jacket and heading to his car.

He'd meant what he'd said about her kids. In just their brief meeting, he could see they were smart and engaging. But he had to school his face to keep away the surprise when the youngsters came up to them. He hadn't expected to meet Rachel's kids. Meeting the kids meant you got further entrenched, and that was not a good thing.

He couldn't say how far this relationship with Rachel was going to go—it was too soon to speculate. He and Rachel weren't getting some happily ever after. He'd had that once, and it had blown up in his face.

But the next man she dated seriously—whenever that

time came—would have his hands full, reigning in that SOB of an ex-husband.

Aside from that, their weekend together was tops. He couldn't remember the last time he'd spent essentially the entire weekend with a woman. Definitely not since Jessica.

He scratched the side of his face.

He should think about watching how much time he spent with Rachel. He couldn't risk her getting too attached. She would hate him when he'd need to split.

Sunday evening and the smile on Rachel's face hadn't faded all weekend. She could tell because her cheeks were starting to hurt. Their first official date country dancing, the kissing, touching, and intimacy. Even the strip club had been a surprising twist of fate.

This year is certainly not like last year!

"Mom, I have another fraction one." Violet broke her stream of thought.

"What's the rule?"

"Turn the second fraction upside down."

"Excellent. Now what?"

"Right! Change the divide into a multiple. Okay, I got it." Her child feverishly wrote, trying to keep up with the speed of her brain.

After dinner, the kids ran upstairs for their allotted electronic time before bed. Rachel had almost finished cleaning the kitchen when her phone rang. *Richie.*

"Rachel, we need to talk." His way of greeting was always so congenial.

She didn't bother to silence her sigh. "Sure. What about?" Like she even needed to ask.

Richie had serious control-freak tendencies. He had no idea that she was dating and likely was more than a little disappointed to learn the way he had—having it paraded before his face.

"I don't know who that man was—"

"His name is Hunter."

"Uh-huh. But I think you need to watch bringing your boyfriends around the kids."

"Okay, sure." She placated him, but it really wasn't any of his business. She never called him when he starting dating Bambi—Brittany—whatever her name was—who was not surprisingly nine years younger than him.

"I'm serious, Rachel. You need to watch yourself."

"Richie, did I call you when you started dating Brittany? No. And as far as what the kids will see, hear, and know about my boyfriends *that* has already been established. So if *you* can follow the rules, then so can I." She shocked herself at how calm and in control she sounded. God, it felt good, even as her heart raced.

"Well—"

"And another thing, when you come to get the kids in two weeks, I want my house key back. It is no longer your house. *You* do not need a key."

"Oh, so the kids and I can wait for you out in the cold. No thanks!"

"Richie, you were early. Furthermore, do I have a key to your place? No, I don't. So return it." Then switching to her sicky-sweet voice, she said, "That's it from my end. Thanks so much for calling." She paused for several beats.

No doubt his jaw had come unhinged, and he was stunned at her new fortitude.

After the silence dragged, she ended the call before he ruined it by opening his mouth.

She breathed out, feeling her shoulders relax. *Wow! That felt good. Why hadn't she done that earlier?*

~

On his third trip to Dallas to meet with the Zeo team Hunter felt optimistic about their progress. He'd had meetings with HR, sales, and lastly the dynamic duo in Marketing. Chanise and Ginny—she insisted he call her that—were getting more comfortable with him. They opened up about business matters, what worked, and what didn't. They joked with him, but also asked thought-provoking questions which told him they were serious about executing on the plan.

As five o'clock quickly approached, Hunter said, "I'm feeling pretty good about our progress, ladies."

They nodded. "I agree," Chanise chimed in.

"So why don't we call it a day? I'd hate to make you late

for happy hour."

They all chuckled, but the ladies exchanged quick glances. "Actually, we were gonna mention that," Ginny said.

"We were planning to head to a bar just down the block for some drinks and appetizers. Care to join us?"

"We won't keep you out late," Ginny kidded.

Building on business relationships was often essential to growing his own company, as well as a way to get referrals. It fell under the old adage: People do business with people they know, like, and trust.

"Sure, sounds good," he replied with a smile.

A short walk down the block they arrived at the bar and grill called Antone's. The place crawled with people just coming from work, laughing, loosening their ties, and letting their hair down on a Thursday night.

Ginny spied a small bar table and stools in the corner. They relaxed into their seats and ordered one round of drinks.

They commenced with basic chit-chat. The ladies were easy to talk to, and Hunter had a repertoire of questions and conversation starters he could pull from anytime he needed to.

"So, Hunter, what do you do for fun?" Ginny asked.

"Well, when I get a break, I like to be active—hiking, biking, running, racquetball—stuff like that."

"Nice, good for you. Being active is important." Ginny sipped on her martini.

Chanise nodded. "Keeps you young." She grinned.

"Speaking of which, should we order some diet jalapeño poppers and low-fat potato skins?"

The ladies laughed at his joke.

The conversation flowed as easily as the liquor. No one had work on the mind. Everyone could relax, and Hunter noticed Chanise and Ginny clasped hands for few beats, like they might be a couple. It didn't bother him in the least, and he knew office relationships happened more than people would ever admit.

Chanise raised her glass. "To healthy, happy lives."

"Here, here." Hunter clinked her glass.

"That's boring." Ginny spoke, but her eyes sparkled. "How about 'to fun since you only live once.'"

"Okay, I'll drink to that too," Hunter clinked her glass.

Chanise leaned forward on the small table bringing her face mere inches from Hunter's. He could make out the golden flecks in her brown eyes. "I have to tell you, Hunter, you're very good at your job."

"Very smart," Ginny agreed.

"Thanks, ladies, I appreciate the compliment."

"You're also very good-looking." Ginny tipped her glass in salute.

Chanise's head snapped in her direction. "You can't say that," she hissed, but the twinkle in her eye told him she held back a smile.

"Oh, he already knows," Ginny replied, her hand gently

stroking his forearm.

Hunter chuckled. His belly vibrated at the motion.

The women joined in on the laughter and the banter was fun. Easy.

"Again, thank you for the compliment."

Ginny leaned forward, meeting his gaze straight-on. Her cupid's bow skated perfectly over her full pink lips. "Hunter, at the risk of stepping outside the bounds of a professional relationship, may I ask you something?"

He lifted a brow. "Okay."

"Have you ever been with two women before?"

His jaw went lax but he quickly slammed it back in place.

In one respect, he was flattered by the attention. And in another, he was surprised at the forwardness of her question. Perhaps Chanise knew it was coming because she didn't scold Ginny for being out of line.

"No, I can't say I have. And if there is an offer on the table, as delightful as that sounds, I am currently seeing someone, so I have to politely decline. For the moment." He added the last part in hopes of softening the blow.

Ginny didn't seem the least bit hurt. "Lucky her. Sad for us, but good for her." She winked before resting back in her stool.

Chanise lifted Ginny's hand to her mouth and kissed it. Both women smiled at each other.

"How long have you two been together?" he asked.

"About two years," Chanise answered.

"Best two years of my life." Ginny sent her a smile.

The evening continued without any additional surprises, because the invitation to a ménage was enough to last for quite a while.

He'd make a mental note to give some distance to the marketing department for the next several weeks.

Honestly, Hunter might have entertained their offer some time ago. Who knows? But the time with Rachel meant something. They may or may not be in a relationship in the traditional sense, but he owed her a level of respect to not date anyone else while he was with her. And frankly, deep inside, he didn't have an interest in another woman right then. Rachel was all he wanted.

~

Nine days had passed with no significant word from Hunter. He'd texted nonsense stuff from the road, and over the weekend as well, mentioning how busy he was.

He did say he would call after his trip.

Rachel was secretly hoping he would want to see her; she could *call* a babysitter after all.

They were supposed to go to San Francisco this weekend—three days away. Shouldn't they at least talk about that, reviewing the plans?

She should be thrilled, but instead she felt sad and empty. She'd been down this road with him before—not hearing from him for days. Then, he'd pop up and they'd have the most incredible fun together. During those times, he would say and do all the right things, like his entire focus was on her.

She sat at her desk, confused, and wondering how to get out of this ridiculous cycle with him. It was distracting to her at work. She knew Roger had an inkling that something was off but kept his opinions to himself.

Hunter seemed to have this push/pull dance he was doing as it pertained to her. They would have a wonderful time together, and just when it looked like they were forming a bond and growing closer, he would step back. Way back. She simply couldn't understand it.

She'd questioned what she did or said. Did she cross some kind of line with him? He was certainly closed off about discussing his marriage or divorce. Could that be the issue? Rachel had given him no indication that she was looking for another husband. No, in fact after the company's ten-year anniversary party, she'd tried to walk away. But he wouldn't let her.

Again—push/pull. And it was making her nuts.

She sighed and jumped when her desk phone rang. "Roger Brennan's office."

"Hi Rachel, it's Patrice in Logistics. Is Roger available?"

"Sure, let me put you through." She put the call on hold and pinged Roger.

"Great. I'll take it," he replied over the phone.

Keeping her mind on work was part of the fallout from the turbulence she had with Hunter.

She pulled on her neck muscles to relieve the tension. If she didn't figure this out soon, she didn't know what she was going to do, because her plan of just going with the flow wasn't working.

Chapter Fourteen

FANTASY. THAT WAS the one word that came into Rachel's head as she entered the five-star hotel in San Francisco. The hotel with its grand lobby of marble tile flooring, pale green fourteen-foot velvet drapes, and a split, curved staircase with brass handrails made her feel like she was in a movie. While married, she and Richie had never taken trips like this, not just the two of them.

She'd flown out alone as Hunter was already there, meeting with his clients.

Rachel had begun to worry when she hadn't heard from him. She'd tried to reassure herself considering she had a plane ticket in her name to join him. But not hearing from him was grueling. Finally, he'd called her.

He'd sounded so excited, so eager to see her. He'd told her he booked a limo to take them to Napa for the whole day Saturday. He'd asked what she was going to bring to wear, which made her a little curious, but otherwise she hadn't given it much thought.

Oh gees. Not that she would confess that to Alexis. If Alexis could have her way, she'd do all of Rachel's packing. At least she had a bunch of new clothes to choose from.

Hunter strode across the lobby, exceptionally handsome in his suit. He stopped in front of her, and with little hesitancy, scooped her up in a deep, passionate kiss. His kiss warmed her instantly from head to toe.

"I'm so glad you're here," he said after a long public display of affection.

She blushed. "Thanks for inviting me."

He lifted her luggage and took her hand, leading her to the elevators. "How was the flight and the cab ride here? Everything good?"

"Yes. Fine. This is a really nice hotel."

He grinned. "It is. I don't often stay here, but since you agreed to come out, I knew I had to book it."

How did he do that? Make her feel so incredibly special when they're together?

The room was decorated just as elegantly as the lobby—crisp white linens, tufted curve-back armchairs, and a breathtaking view of downtown and the Golden Gate Bridge in the distance.

"We have dinner reservations in two hours at the top-floor restaurant." He hoisted her luggage onto the bench and met her at the window looking out.

"That sounds great."

He helped her out of her coat and laid it on the back of a chair. He took off his suit jacket and added it to the pile, then slipped off his striped tie, setting loose his top button.

He reached for her hand, and kissing the wrist, laid it against his chest. Cupping her cheek with the other, he smoothed her lower lip with his thumb. "I was thinking about taking a shower. Care to join me?"

He smelled so good standing this close, a woodsy masculine scent. How interesting, she thought, what little attention I paid to the scent of a man or his cologne, until Hunter. And now, she could get drunk on it.

"Okay," she breathed out.

His hands stroked her arms, making their way to her abdomen under her sweater. The contact with her bare skin sent tingles throughout her body. He clasped the hem of her sweater and pulled it over her head. He grinned as she started on his shirt buttons and pants. In no time, they were stripped down to their undergarments—the outline of his delicious cock evident in his boxer briefs.

Hunter took her hand and led her to the bedroom.

She grabbed her makeup bag from her luggage to fish out a clip for her hair and dropped the last of her clothing on the bathroom floor.

Letting him lead the way, she stepped into the shower area and instantly the hot water covered her. So did his hands.

Oh God, his caresses were like heaven. How she missed

this.

"I can't go two weeks without fucking you, Rachel. It nearly killed me," he whispered from behind her as he peppered kisses along her neck. His hands toyed with her breasts and nipples, and the ache at her sex intensified.

He stopped and grabbed a washcloth, loading it with the hotel-supplied body wash. Starting at her back, he stroked gentle circles with his left hand as his right arm caressed her front. He worked her entire backside, then squirted more on his palm. "Spread your legs, baby."

She placed a hand on the wall for balance and widened her stance.

His palm circled her ass cheek before creeping to the center. His fingers skated down her crevice and over her tiny hole.

"Oh," she breathed out.

His gentle movements were so exhilarating and perhaps erotic because it felt forbidden.

"Turn around."

She pivoted to face him.

He repeated the cleansing on her front as the spray rinsed her back.

Stroking her breasts, her legs, fondling her sex, it all felt so incredible. Heat filled her cheeks as the slickness grew between her legs.

He stood, dropped the washcloth, and claimed her mouth. Their mouths fused in a tangle of lips and tongues.

"Rinse, beautiful, then put both hands on the wall."

Yes!

She did as he bid and rested her palms on the tile, presenting him with her back, keeping her legs apart.

He gripped her hips and pulled her back several inches. His rock-solid cock slid easily through her wet slit.

"Ah." She waited for him to enter, but he didn't. Water continued to pound them.

She glanced back and, as he massaged her ass cheeks, he slid down low—his mouth at her buttocks.

Oh God, was all she could think.

Hunter kissed and licked her cheeks, the ache building to unbearable levels.

Then without ceremony, he gripped her cheeks, taking them wide, and laid claim to her backside.

"Oh," she cried out. The sensation was simply exquisite. "Oh God, Hunter." She shouldn't like this. Her head dropped back as he continued his delicious torture.

His thumbs glossed underneath to find her lips and clit. He easily slid a thumb inside her, stimulating the first few inches of her channel, as the other thumb circled over her clit.

"Oh. Oh, Hunter." She couldn't think. She was delirious on lust and passion. The sensations piled one on top of the other, building an insane crescendo of pleasure. She arched her back for him. He growled against her.

The incredible buildup finally exploded, sending pleasure rocketing to every pore in her body. She shrieked, trying desperately not to scream in the hotel.

As she calmed down, he laid kisses over her backside. Out of the corner of her eye, she saw Hunter reach for a condom.

In mere seconds, he was sheathed, and hands holding her hips, he dove into her from behind.

He groaned. "God, Rachel. You feel so good." He moaned as he pumped into her.

"Mmm."

He came, and she knew this was just the beginning of their weekend together. She wondered how many times he would want to make love. She craved it. God, how she craved it. She wanted everything with Hunter.

Chapter Fifteen

HUNTER BASKED IN the glorious day he had with Rachel—walking among the vineyards, sampling wines, eating lunch at one of the oldest restaurants in the valley. He loved watching her eyes light up with just about every new taste that hit her tongue.

If Hunter was a betting man, he'd bet her ex-husband never took her anywhere. Served him right. He'd lost probably the best thing that ever happened to him. Lucky for Hunter because at least for the foreseeable future, she was his.

Now she rested her head against his shoulder in the back of the limo, reminiscing over the day as well.

"So how many bottles did you end up buying?" she asked.

"Well, I'm having three cases sent home, so thirty-six there, and I've purchased four bottles to check in my luggage."

"Nice." She glanced up at him quickly. "I have a pretty good wine collection at the house."

"You do?"

She nodded. "Maybe you can come over some time for dinner. I can show it to you."

He swallowed hard. He had an inkling of what she was asking for—a relationship. She wanted more.

He kissed the top of her head. He wasn't equipped for something like that. Sex he could do, a relationship wasn't possible.

In fact now, with the scent of her subtle lavender shampoo lingering—so fitting for her, innocent and pure—he had thoughts far from innocent and pure. The limo had a partition in addition to tinted windows.

Nestled close to him, she was simply too lovely to resist. Forget that he'd had her that morning and twice the night before.

With his finger, he lifted her lips to his.

She sighed.

He claimed more as she opened for him. He could still taste the Bordeaux on her lips. Caressing her jaw and neck, he let his fingertips dip to the tip of her cleavage just under her V-neck sweater.

She shifted in her seat but didn't pull away.

He slid the arm resting around her shoulders down her back circling her waist. Pulling her close, the press of her breasts against him was enough to drive him mad.

He had to have her, and he hoped she'd let him.

Breaking the kiss, he stretched his arm and triggered the partition behind the driver to raise. They were in complete privacy.

"Rachel, you know I find it hard to keep my hands off you. We have absolute privacy right now, and the drive is over an hour before we reach the hotel. Will you let me ravish you?"

Her eyes rounded to saucers.

He had no doubt shocked her. Her adorable expressions seared in his mind. He wanted so much from her and wanted to give her so much. At least give her body so much. *Please say yes.*

"Here?" she whispered.

"Yes, baby. The driver can't see or hear us. No one can." At least he didn't think the driver could hear them.

"I'm wearing pants."

"I know. I want to slide them off you. I want to make you feel good." He lifted her hand and slid it over his raging hard-on. "I crave you constantly, Rachel. Since the moment you burst out of Roger's office, thoughts of you have filled my days."

Her jaw gaped.

He pressed on, lavishing kisses on her lips and neck, nibbling and sucking, while he loosened the button and zipper of her pants.

He counted on the residual from the wine tastings still

pulsing through her veins, lowering her inhibitions enough for him to have her.

She didn't stop him.

He loved that she was open to new things. He shifted them, laying her down on the long bench. Pushing her sweater up, he claimed her soft warm skin with his mouth. Wasting no time, he flicked her bra from behind, then grabbed it with her top, pulling over her head, tossing them to the floor.

Her full, teardrop breasts called to him. *God.* He laved and toyed with her dark, rosy nubs while she squirmed below him. Her delicate scent slowly filled the backseat.

With two hands, he gripped her pants and panties and yanked them to her ankles. Quickly, he flung off her shoe so he could free one leg. He bent her leg and rested her foot on the bench as he lowered to the floor to taste her sweet fruit.

"Unh," she cried out in surprise.

Her fingers laced through his hair as he circled her tiny bud. She lifted her hips, trying to get closer to the source of pleasure.

"Hunter." Her voice was breathy and heavy with lust.

He wanted to hear her scream out her orgasm. Maybe he'd have time to give her more than one.

She became quiet. He knew that meant she was on the verge of climaxing. He lessened the pressure on her clit. She whimpered.

"Hang on, baby." He reached in his back pocket for a

condom, raised his head, and handed it to her. "Put this on me."

As she shifted, he took a seat, and slouching, he loosened his pants, giving her access to him.

Her eyes positively sparkled.

Hunter had come to one very solid conclusion: it had been a long time since Rachel had been with a man who knew how to please her. How to worship her in a way she deserved.

She rolled on the condom and took the hand he offered. Straddling him, she held him and lowered herself.

"Fuuck." She felt like heaven wrapped around him.

He ravished her mouth, plumbing the depths as she rocked over him. God, he couldn't get enough of her.

"Now, lean back, baby. Hands on my knees."

She arched and gripped his knees for support. Her beautiful naked body was a feast for his eyes.

He smoothed over her hard clit, and her muscles clenched him.

Gently circling, he reached his free hand for her breasts. Her creamy skin topped with rosy nipples, he toyed and twisted, causing her to moan.

He would let her rise again and keep her on the edge. When he felt her muscles flutter, he stopped. He grabbed both her hands behind her back and, clasping her neck, brought her mouth to his.

"Hunter, please," she breathed over his lips.

He flexed his muscles to stave off his own orgasm. Not

yet. He wanted her to explode like she never had before. He wanted to make a mess; he didn't care if he was charged an added fee. She was his woman, his to worship and adore.

He broke the kiss and pushed her gorgeous breasts to his mouth then he sucked in hard, as much as he could.

She shrieked.

The more he played with her breasts, the more she squirmed over him. He loved to see her on the brink of ecstasy.

"What do you want, baby?"

"Please. I need to come."

"You will." Hunter thrust into her. He released her hands and returned to her needy clit. Several small circles later, she panted and moaned, her inner muscles twitching around him.

"Ah!" she cried out as her head fell back and her spine bowed.

Gripping her hips, he thrust as deeply as he could, ramming in to the end of her, detonating another orgasm and finally releasing his own.

The climax seemed to go on forever—her warmth surrounding him, making him feel like he wanted her forever, even if it was impossible.

As the fog started to clear, Rachel panted lightly in the crux of his neck, her hands resting on his shoulders. "Ohmigosh."

He kissed her temple. "You were amazing, baby."

"I'm quite sure the driver heard me."

"Doesn't matter. He gets paid not to hear you."

She smiled against his skin.

He kissed her again, holding her close, caressing her back and wondering how he would ever be able to let her go.

Chapter Sixteen

THE PAST THREE months had been spectacular, for the most part. The hardest times were not hearing from Hunter. She knew his travel made it a challenge to get together.

Maybe Rachel was kidding herself, but she couldn't remember a time in her life when she'd felt more alive—nature looked prettier, color became brighter, and everyone seemed friendlier. She'd even lost a few pounds. Alexis had said, *Sex becomes you.*

She still chuckled over that one.

Lexi had a point. Just the week prior, Hunter had invited her to his apartment for dinner. She'd been greeted immediately with a passionate kiss. She'd worn a lightweight raincoat, and he'd asked her to keep it on and follow him. The gleam in his eyes told her he might have something titillating in mind.

She'd dressed in a long-sleeved knit top, boots, and a

straight wool skirt that curved over her ass perfectly. Leaving her purse on his sofa, she'd held his hand and followed him to the elevator. He'd pressed the button for the top floor. They'd walked down the hall to a door tucked in the corner labeled Roof.

She'd swallowed hard but didn't stop. Couldn't stop.

The view at night of downtown Houston had been stunning—clear skies and visibility for miles. A thousand lights sprinkled across the skyline. They'd walked along the flat roof taking in the three-sixty view. The building owners had finished the rooftop nicely with chairs and loungers, potted plants, and artificial turf.

Hunter had stopped her at the north end, next to the railing. Pulling her close, his arm went underneath her long coat, and he'd claimed her lips in another passionate kiss. His erection dug into her low belly. He'd felt so warm, she simply melted into him.

His hand skated down her back, cupping her ass. He'd whispered over her lips, "I had a fantasy. Of you and me up here."

She tilted her head back, meeting his gaze. "You did?"

He nodded. "I know for a fact they don't have cameras installed up here yet, so you don't have to worry about that. And your coat will hide a lot, I'll make sure of it." He laid kisses down her neck. "Let me have you here, baby. Let me fuck you."

His words had sent a shiver racing through her body.

She'd moaned as his hands wandered up to her breasts, massaging the flesh and toying with her nipples. Her breaths came harder.

He'd slowly backed them up to the brick wall in the middle of the rooftop. He bent his knees to lower before her.

Oh God, she was going to do this. She was going to let him do this to her outside. Her willpower vanished. Gone were the days of Guarded Rachel.

His hands slid up under her skirt to her thong. His thumb skated over her clitoris while his fingers stroked along her crevice, dampening her panties further.

She'd slammed her hands against the wall to keep her balance.

He'd dragged her thong down her legs and over her boots. And with little finesse, he pushed her skirt up over her hips, exposing her sex to his warm, wet tongue.

"Oh God."

He'd ravaged her like a starving man, laying claim to her, taking what he wanted and leaving her with only pleasure.

Her hips flexed into his face, feeling the impending climb.

Then, he'd stopped.

What?!

He'd straightened and unfastened his jeans. Ripping open a condom he'd pulled from his pocket, he sheathed himself.

Rachel's gaze had dashed to the right and the left one last time, praying no one could see because she desperately needed him to finish what he'd started.

"Baby, I want a taste." As he spoke, he'd gently pushed up her top and pulled against her bra cups, letting her breasts spring free. He wasted no time sucking a nipple into his mouth while he played with the other.

She moaned. Every time Hunter played with her nipples they became more sensitive, sending delicious electricity throughout her body.

He'd lifted his head and swung them around so his back leaned against the wall. One arm wrapped around her waist, the other lifted her left leg, effectively aligning her pussy to him. "Baby, help me. Put me inside you."

She'd reached for his thick, throbbing girth and settled over him.

"Fuck, baby," he whispered over her lips.

He'd pumped into her, her nipples scraping against his shirt.

The climax that had been ready to release started its ascent again. She craved him holding her close, stroking her core, kissing her deeply. When she was with Hunter, she felt like the Queen of the Universe.

"Baby, come with me. Play with your clit. I want to feel you squeeze my cock deeper inside you."

She'd slipped her hand down between them to her eager clit and circled it several times. Her inner muscles flexed.

"That's right, baby. So close."

In another second, she exploded, followed shortly by him. He growled in her ear and panted in her neck as he thrust out the last of his seed.

"Holy fuck, baby. That was incredible."

They'd put themselves back together and made their way downstairs to his apartment, still flush from their sexcapade. They laughed about it, and he admitted he'd like to do that again when the weather was warmer so she could wear less clothing.

Oh gees! She didn't know about that.

But as she freshened her makeup at the bathroom mirror, waiting for Hunter to pick her up for dinner at Romano's, the thought crept into her head once again.

Despite herself, deep inside she knew this was more than *just sex*. She'd fallen in love with him. She could no longer deny it.

Sure, it was great sex, but there was a connection between them. And she was certain he knew it too. Their laughter, their banter, when they held hands, when he asked about her day—all the different ways he showed how much he cared told her he loved her too.

But could he see that with the wall he'd built around himself?

Sitting in a booth at Romano's, enjoying the escargot appetizer, Rachel knew this was supposed to be a "normal" date, like the other dates they'd had.

But she had to say something; it was killing her to keep her feelings inside.

She felt Hunter was holding back, and she didn't know why. She didn't know what to say, but she had to try. She could see a future with this man, if that's what he wanted. And right now, she wasn't so sure he did.

"Hunter, can we talk about something?"

He nodded, a reserved sparkle in his eyes. "Sure."

"I'd been thinking a lot about this lately. You have this confidence, like you don't have a care in the world. And yet, part of you seems so unapproachable. Like you're protecting yourself."

Something dark flashed through his gaze before it became distant, as did his body language.

See, that's what I'm talking about.

He seemed to close himself off when the topic got too hot to handle. She'd definitely touched on a nerve.

She patiently waited for him to comment. After several long beats of silence, she asked softly, "What is it?"

He inhaled, shifting in his chair slightly. "It's about my wife." He briefly made eye contact with her.

She studied the table in confusion. "I thought you were divorced. That it was a bad divorce and that's why you didn't want to talk about it." *Is he still freakin' married?*

Hunter ran a hand across his jaw and down the back of

his neck. He could no longer keep it from her. Rachel deserved to hear the truth. At the very least, he owed her that.

"No, I'm sorry I misled you. But that's not the truth." He didn't like talking about his wife's death. It was the darkest time of his life. Pushing it away from his thoughts had helped him to deal with the tragedy. Keeping his emotional distance from Rachel would ensure she'd never be touched by the same darkness that still lived inside him.

"My wife, Jessica, had a sister with a drug problem. Jessica happened to be at Marie's apartment when her drug dealer showed up. They were standing by the door, arguing. Jessica tried to calm them down, but it did no good. He ended up pulling out a gun and Jessica stood between him and Marie. She took the bullet."

Rachel gasped. "Oh, I'm so sorry, Hunter. How long ago was this?"

"Eight years ago. She died in the hospital."

"How horrible. I'm so sorry."

He stared out into the distance. "I was definitely in shock. For weeks, I felt like I was just going through the motions of life." The emotion was still raw, like it had happened yesterday. "My business wasn't as busy as it is now, and maybe that was a blessing because I was just doing the bare minimum."

"That's understandable." She rested a hand over his. "I can't imagine what you must have gone through."

"Jessica and I had talked about kids someday, places

we'd like to travel to..." He blotted a finger over his upper lip. "My sister and mother helped me donate her things, and I just immersed myself in work."

"What about Marie? Was she hurt?"

His blood pressure skyrocketed at the mere mention of her name.

He shook his head. "No. And I don't have much to say about her."

Rachel had stopped eating; they both had. He wished they could drop the subject completely.

A silence fell over the table, then Rachel asked, "Do you talk to Marie anymore?"

"Rachel, because of her selfishness, her lack of maturity, and her stupid addiction, my wife was gone." His happily ever after had vanished into thin air that day.

"I get that. I bet she feels bad too." Rachel glanced down at her plate of food getting cold.

Now it was his turn to cup his hand around hers. "Rach, can we get back to eating?"

She tilted her head. "It seems to me you throw yourself into your work to forget. And maybe building business connections helps you to avoid the personal ones?"

He sipped his ice water. "I hadn't really thought about it."

"Do you think you're still holding on to some blame and resentment?"

"You sound like my family."

She bit her lip. "All that emotion is holding you back."

His back stiffened, and he pulled his arm off the table. "You think I should just forgive her?"

"I'm just suggesting maybe you have to sorta face what happened, if you want a future with someone."

Rachel smoothed her lips together and inhaled. She looked as if she was searching for her next words. He tried not to get defensive about it, but dammit, because of that druggie his wife was dead. *No one* could just forgive and forget.

"I...I can feel a wall around you, Hunter." Her eyes lost their sparkle. "At first I thought it was maybe me or the kids. But in the time we've been together, I've gotten glimpses of you. You without your barriers up—playful, carefree, loving. And during that time, I've fallen in love with you."

What?! No, that can't happen.

He was not the right man for her to fall in love with. He would never be whole. She could do so much better.

Rachel brushed her hands over the cloth napkin in her lap. "You may not agree with me, but I see a future for us." She shrugged her shoulders. "But I want the real, authentic you. Ya know?"

He pursed his lips together. "Rachel...I don't know if I can do the happily ever after stuff. I thought you knew that."

A tear streamed down her cheek. "Yes, perhaps I did. Or maybe the feelings I have for you have simply blown all caution away."

What could he say? She'd just professed her love for him, and he couldn't return it. Not in this lifetime. *Fuck!*

His chance at happily ever after had come and gone.

Rachel reached for her purse. "Well, at least you know how I feel. You know where to find me if you change your mind." She rose, her skin ruddy. "Take care, Hunter." She leaned down and kissed his cheek, then quickly spun around and headed for the door.

She was leaving him—left him. This was supposed to be a date, like the many they'd had before. Why couldn't they just date?

It was too good to be true.

Fuck! He might have just screwed up everything.

Chapter Seventeen

RACHEL KEPT IT together until she got outside the restaurant, forcing her legs to move. "Please call me a cab," she managed to squeak out to the valet.

It felt like an eternity, but the cab came around the corner, and she collapsed in the back seat, relaying her home address.

"Oh God," she breathed out as the tears streamed down her face.

She had to leave him there, right? She had to have a clean break. There would never be a good time. The more she stayed with him, the harder it would be to separate.

She wanted Hunter, all of him, not just pieces of what he'd shown her. Her heart ached for the loss of his wife, and what that must have been like. But she could be there for him, help him heal. She *wanted* to be there for him. But he wasn't letting her in.

She paid the driver and walked inside her house. She

dialed Alexis.

"Hello?"

"Lexi." A sob escaped.

"Oh God, what's wrong?"

"Hunter."

"I'll be right over."

Rachel sat on the sofa, numb. She didn't have to hide a thing since the kids were at Richie's.

About twenty minutes later, a soft knock came at the door, and Lexi opened it. A frown pulled at her lips. She came to Rachel, sat beside her, and wrapped her arms around her.

Rachel released a torrent of tears, sobbing into her hands as her friend held her tight.

After several minutes, she composed herself enough to retell Lexi the story.

"I did the right thing, didn't I? I had to get up and leave. I can't stay when there's no future."

Lexi sighed. "I know you've been struggling with this for a while. This explains a lot."

"It really does. I don't want to sound uncaring. I *want* to be there for him, but he won't let me in. And it kills me. Part of him is living in the past." She blotted her tears with her beaten tissue. "I love him, Lexi. I wish I hadn't fallen for him, but I did. Now what I am I gonna do?"

Her friend smoothed a hand over her back. Just her presence soothed Rachel. "Let me make you some chamomile tea so you can get some sleep. Things will be in perspective in the morning."

Rachel nodded. She doubted she would feel any better in the morning, but the tea would be good. She replayed the evening in her mind, the way Hunter tensed talking about his former wife. The emotion raging behind those eyes told of the pain he'd been living with. He'd been carrying this burden for eight long years. Bless his soul.

She wanted to comfort him, to tell him everything would be all right, but he wasn't ready to hear that. He had to reconcile the past before they could have a future. And God, she prayed they could have a future.

Hunter sat at the desk in his home office, forcing himself to chip away at his To Do list. But really, all he was doing was pushing paper around.

Another week had passed, and the ache in Hunter's gut hadn't subsided. He knew he had no one to blame but himself. He'd let Rachel walk out of his life, and now he was miserable.

He missed her the exact same way he'd missed Jessica all those years ago. The kicker was he could see all he'd been missing when he was with Rachel—the dancing, the kids, the intimacy. He wanted to be with her as equally as he didn't.

His sister Janet called to chat and he wished he was in the mood. Frankly, nothing felt right in his world. He hoped with time things would get better.

Minutes after a conversation with his sister, his phone rang. His mother. He shouldn't have been surprised. His sister had a sixth sense, always had. She could tell something was off.

"Hi, Mom."

"Hey, Hunter. How are you? Janet called and mentioned you don't sound like yourself. What's going on?"

He sighed. He'd been doing a lot of that lately. "Mom, I'm fine."

"No, you're not. I can tell. Is it work or... a woman?"

His mother was a champion at asking leading questions—a skill Hunter also successfully implemented in his job.

But how could he explain what bounced around in his head, kept him up at night, when he didn't exactly know himself?

"It's hard to explain."

"Try."

"I met a woman a few months ago, and things seemed to be going well, but—I don't know. She wants more."

"And you're not prepared to give it to her?" It was a question she knew the answer to—his whole family knew.

"I suppose not, but things were going just fine the way they were. Great, actually."

"So, why do you think you don't want more with this woman? Is she good to you?"

Thoughts of Rachel smiling at him, laughing with him,

her arms wrapped around him, made his heart twinge. He missed her more than words could describe. "She's the best, Mom."

He recounted the story of dinner with Rachel.

"You know what I think? You need to talk to Marie."

He blinked, and his heart skipped a beat. "Why would I do that?"

"Because you need to forgive her. It's poison not forgiving her. You have to move on. You're gonna lose your one chance to be happy again. Why are you holding on to this anger? It's like two people dying. You're alive, but you might as well be dead inside."

Silence stretched over the phone.

He scratched the back of his neck. "I don't know, Mom."

"Marie didn't pull the trigger, Hunter. And remember, she had her own demons. She has guilt over this too. By you holding on to this anger, you're making it worse."

Could his mother be right? He was making it worse?

Her voice softened as she said, "Hunter, promise me, you'll talk to her. You owe it to yourself, *and* you owe it to Jessica."

His mind raced. Now, hours after the call with his mother had ended, her words still replayed in his head. He struggled to focus on work. To focus on anything really.

Was she right?

Fuck!

He didn't want to talk to that woman. The thought made

him want to throw up his lunch. But he knew *because* he didn't want to talk to her, something was wrong and he needed to attack it head-on.

He blew out a breath.

~

The following day, Saturday, he waited on the porch of Marie's two-story home in a suburb of Houston. His mother had given him the address.

He couldn't bring himself to knock.

"Hello?" a child's voice sounded from behind him.

Hunter spun around.

The boy bent down and lifted his skateboard before climbing the two steps to meet Hunter where he stood.

"Can I help you?"

The boy couldn't be older than seven with brown wavy hair and bright eyes looking up at him. He reminded Hunter of Rachel's boy.

"Do you live here?"

"Yeah."

"I came to talk to your mom."

"Okay."

He powered by Hunter and opened the front door. "C'mon." He looked back at Hunter.

Hunter stayed put.

"Mom!" the boy called out.

"In here."

A faint smell of cinnamon hung in the air as Hunter entered the house.

A woman stood in the kitchen, arranging and examining paint chips on the island. She looked so much like Jessica, similar build and the same dark blonde hair. This woman had a glow to her skin Hunter had never seen in her before.

"There's someone here to see you," the boy announced.

She looked at her son, then quickly her eyes darted to him. They widened. "Oh."

The pause told Hunter he was the last person she'd expected to see.

"Hi." Marie straightened. "Okay, Bobby. You can go back outside."

The boy scowled up at him but then decided that Hunter was all right. "Bye." He took off for the front door, back to whatever he was doing before Hunter had arrived.

"What are you doing here?" Marie asked with reservation in her voice.

"It's been a while. Uh, you have a nice boy there." He motioned with his head toward the front.

The corners of her mouth curved upward. "Thanks."

Hunter licked his lips, useless when his mouth was so dry. "I wanted to talk to you. We never really discussed what happened."

The sparkle in Marie's eyes faded. "Okay."

He knew that was his cue to start talking, but damn if he knew what to say. "I still think about her. I miss her sometimes." He rested his hands on the cold granite countertop as a tightness settled in his chest. He and Jessica had had a connection that was supposed to last a lifetime. His brain knew she was gone, but his heart struggled to process that fact.

Marie's lips pulled into a frown. "Me too." On an exhale, she continued, "She saved my life."

Hunter knew that and somehow hearing it from Marie made him proud of Jessica. Proud to have been her husband. "I don't..." He tried gathering his thoughts. "You look good. Healthy."

Marie tilted her head. "Thanks." She tapped the counter. "Hunter, I'm sure this is hard for you." She exhaled. "I've been clean since then. I've done a complete one-eighty. I got married, and as you can see, we have a son." Her eyes glistened with unshed tears. "In a way, I owe it all to Jessica. She helped me turn my life around."

Hunter could see that Marie lived a good life now.

"Marie, I'm trying to come to terms with all this. I know that sounds foolish, after all these years, but I think I'm holding onto some anger. I blamed you."

She swallowed, and a tear slid down her cheek. "It takes time. I was angry with myself. Jess meant the world to me, and I was responsible for ending her life."

What? He hid the surprise he felt inside.

"There wasn't a day that went by that I didn't think about her, Hunter. I worked to forgive myself and move forward."

His neck muscles tightened. "You can't beat yourself up. You didn't pull the trigger."

Did he really just say that?

Her eyes rounded.

"I just...I don't want to hang on to this anger anymore."

Another tear escaped. "Then don't. Please don't. Jessica would want you to move on. Find someone to share the rest of your life with."

Her words washed over him. "I think she would."

She shifted her weight to one hip. "Have you met someone?"

Rachel's smiling face flashed in his mind. The corner of his mouth pulled upward. "I think I have. But I may have chased her away."

Marie shook her head repeatedly. "No. No, Hunter. It's never too late. Please trust me. You can fix this."

He met her eyes. Tears streaked down her cheeks.

He licked his lips and glanced down at the array of paint chips on the counter. "Are you painting?"

She pushed back a stack of paint selections. "Yes. It's time for a new paint color. At least the inside of the house."

He perused the chips and pointed to the pale buttercream yellow. "That's a good one. Jessica would have said to put this in a room with a northern exposure."

Having been an artist, his wife had an incredible eye for color. The thought brought a lightness to his heart.

"Yeah." Marie grinned, probably having the same fond memory. "That would be nice."

He walked to the other side of the island and put his arms around Marie. It felt awkward at first, but he settled into it. This was his wife's sister, she was family.

"Thanks for talking to me." He released her after a moment. Her eyes filled with tears again. "Take care of yourself."

"You too, Hunter."

Marie escorted him out the front door where Bobby was practicing jumping the curb with his skateboard.

Whap!

Hunter could see the frustration in his scrunched-up face when he plopped to the pavement.

Walking to his car, he called out, "Bobby, try and lift up the front leg a bit and put more weight on the back leg."

Bobby pushed his helmet back and lifted his board to try again.

Hunter waited to see how the boy did. His nephew.

Gaining some speed, Bobby sailed to the curb, and working his legs, he got some air and landed smoothly on the cul de sac. He rolled back around to face Hunter, grinning from ear to ear. "It worked!"

"There ya' go. More practice and you might need to build a ramp."

The boy's eyes lit up, and he looked at his mom.

Marie, watching from the porch, shook her head, but

her lips tugged up at the corners.

Hunter backed his car out of the driveway, sending one last look to Bobby who waved to him.

The lightness in his car was vastly different than what he'd felt driving to Marie's. She looked good, healthy, and it was clear she'd turned her life around. And yes, Jessica had done that. That was Jessica's legacy.

Hunter felt a wave of peace flow over him that he hadn't felt in a very long time. His mom was right; he'd needed to talk to Marie to move past this. Somehow seeing her helped him to close that chapter of his life. He might still miss Jessica now and again, but he had life left to live.

He'd thought he *was* living his life, but now he could admit he wasn't. And perhaps the one thing missing most was a sweet, blue-eyed blonde with two smart kids and passion for encouraging and nurturing those around her.

He only hoped he wasn't too late.

Chapter Eighteen

THE DOORBELL RANG. Rachel wasn't expecting anyone. She'd hope it was Hunter but knew better than to waste her energy on wishful thinking. It had been two weeks since she'd seen him.

She slipped off her rubber gloves from cleaning the pots when Lexi rose off the barstool. "I'll get it."

She had invited her friend over for dinner—it was a weekly ritual—but now it was even more important with how lousy she was feeling over Hunter.

"It's probably Girl Scouts, but I'm good. I already have four boxes in the pantry."

Her friend grinned and made her way to the front door.

Lexi greeted whoever was there, her voice noticeably higher and welcoming. That didn't sound like Girl Scouts.

Seconds later, Lexi returned, Hunter standing by her side.

Rachel's jaw gaped, but shock blocked her brain and she

couldn't close it.

"So, I'm gonna go check on the kids," Lexi announced, making direct eye contact with her, as if to make sure that was what she wanted before leaving.

"Thanks," she murmured.

"Hi." Hunter's gaze penetrated her mind and body. Him standing before her in her kitchen was surreal.

She'd missed him so bad it ached. "Hi."

"I'm sorry I didn't call, but I had to see you."

"It's all right." He could wake her in the dead of night, if he had to.

"Um," he glanced at the staircase where Lexi had just gone. "Is there a chance we can go for a drive? Maybe talk?"

He wanted to leave. Sure, that made sense. Lexi and her kids were around. She wondered what he wanted to talk about. But if it was friends with benefits he wanted, she couldn't do that. Her heart had fallen for him, and she just couldn't settle.

In a beat, the kids barreled down the stairs, followed by Lexi. "We're gonna run out for ice cream. We'll be back in about an hour."

"Can we go, Mom?" Violet's eyes sparkled in excitement.

"Sure. Have fun."

"Hi, Mr. Hunter. Bye, Mr. Hunter," the kids called.

Out the front door the kids went. Lexi sent her a wink as she grabbed her purse and closed the door behind her.

"So, I guess we don't have to go anywhere." She forced a

little smile.

Her heart pounded in her chest. Was he there to say goodbye or to try and win her back? The way he looked down and bit on the inside of his cheek told her this might not be what she wanted to hear.

And, God, she didn't know if she could handle that.

He took a step closer, leaning a hip against the counter, a foot from her. "For years, I'd convinced myself I was living my best life. That it was a full and satisfying life. Growing my business and connecting with people was my yardstick. It wasn't until you that I realized I've been lying to myself."

She held her breath.

"Rachel," he reached for her hand and cupped it. "Before, I couldn't see a future. Now, I know where I want it to go." He squeezed her fingers. "Anger blinded me from the truth. How could I have not seen it? Why was I fighting it so hard?"

She couldn't quite follow him. It was like she was hearing part of a conversation he'd already had with himself. "Hunter, I'm having trouble understanding what you're telling me."

He moved closer, inches from her, and clasped both her hands between them. "Right, I'm sorry." He shook his head. "Rachel, meeting you turned my world upside down. In a good way. I didn't think I could be happy again after I lost Jessica. But I'm miserable without you."

She swallowed, feeling tears prick her eyes.

Holding her gaze, he skimmed a thumb along her cheek and jaw. "I've loved two women in my life. One has passed, but one is right here. And I'll be damned if I'm going to let her go."

"Oh, God," she whispered. A droplet escaped—those were the words she'd ached to hear.

"I'm not perfect, baby, but if you're willing to give me a chance, I'll work my hardest to make you happy." With a thumb, he swept away her tears.

"I was miserable without you too."

He leaned down to kiss her, softly at first, then more insistent, more urgent, cupping the back of her neck.

He felt so good, his body pressed against hers. She hadn't known she'd ever feel his lips again, or see his smile, know his touch.

He pulled back, and the warmth between them simmered.

"Rachel, I know you want all of me, and I may have more healing to do, but I'll fight for it every day. I want all of you."

"You have it." She smiled wide...this was her dream come true.

He shook his head, and her smile faltered.

"The only way I can ensure I have all of you is to marry you." He wrapped an arm around her waist and crushed her into his frame. "Marry me, Rachel. Give me a second chance at love. Give us a second chance."

The tears chased each other down her cheeks. She

grasped the back of his neck and breathed, "Yes," just before she kissed him.

His arms lifted her, his mouth making all kinds of demands on hers.

"I want you now, baby. On this counter or in your bed."

"Bed." She pointed him in the right direction.

He set her down beside her king-size bed, lifting her T-shirt off in the same motion. Then he pulled his own off. She worked his jeans loose, followed by hers. Shoes went sailing.

She unclasped her bra and breathed in his glorious scent as he pulled her flush to his naked body.

Skin to skin, they lay down on the bed, the weight of this wonderful man encapsulating her, possessing her.

He claimed her mouth again like he couldn't get enough. He reached for her thigh, bringing her leg beside his as he caressed her hip.

"I'm helplessly in love with you, Rachel." His lips traveled down her neck to her breasts, leaving a hot trail in its wake. "I can't get enough of you."

She moaned when his lips closed on her taut nipple, nibbling and sucking, sending delicious energy straight south.

"I love you, Hunter." She was swept away with emotion, the weeks of misery finally laid to rest. And she'd just agreed to marry this man.

His mouth moved to her belly, covering her torso with kisses.

Wait! Her mind raced—she couldn't go back to how it was. It would kill her.

She clasped his head to stop him. He raised his eyes to hers. "Hunter, when you go away for business—"

"I know." His eyebrows pinched together. "I ignore you. And I'm sorry. That won't be happening anymore. I'll be calling you regularly." A hand slipped between them, and a finger found its way to her slit. "You'll never wonder if you're on my mind. You'll never wonder if I'd rather be holding you, sharing stories with you," and in a smooth motion, pulling her panties aside, his bare erection dove into her, "or making love to you."

"Unh." Her back bowed off the bed at the exquisite sensation.

Slowly, as if savoring every push and pull, he made love to her like he never had before. His mouth covered hers, his tongue consumed her. She rode the waves of their sensual journey, slowly climbing higher.

Lifting onto a forearm, he kept her gaze as he slowly pumped into her, gently stimulating her clit at the same time.

She was going mad on the deliciousness of it. "Hunter. God, Hunter." Her eyes fluttered closed, but he didn't yield— not any faster or any slower—just dangling her on the edge of ecstasy.

"You're mine, Rachel." Still, he pumped slowly. "I'll spend the rest of my life making you happy."

"Ah." She could feel the emotion—the love *and* the

lust—wash over her. She climbed higher. She writhed, but it did no good. Hunter held her pleasure, all her pleasure.

"I am yours...and you...are mine."

"That's right, baby," he whispered over her lips as he drove in deeper and stronger.

Just those few perfect thrusts had them both coming. She screamed his name, not even knowing her own.

He spilled into her, rocking with her and kissing her face and neck, whispering, "I love you. I love you."

Finally, the wave ebbed, and he collapsed over her. She wrapped him in her arms and legs, relishing the feel of the man she loved more than she loved herself.

In a few short moments, he strode to the bathroom to retrieve a washcloth to clean her up. Then he slipped them under the covers and pulled her close. "How much time do you think we have left?"

She glanced at her watch. "Maybe twenty minutes."

"Good." He wiggled his brows. "We might have time for round two."

Rachel chuckled. "Oh, no you don't." She pecked his lips, but pushed against is chest, mockingly holding him off her.

He smiled. "Can I take you and the kids out for dinner this weekend?"

Her heart skipped a beat at his request. "Yes, that would be lovely."

"I know a place. Have you ever been to Sweet Sophia's?"

She shook her head. "Can't say that I have."

"Perfect. You'll love it. Incredible spareribs and garlic mashed potatoes."

Her smile fell.

"What is it?"

"Um, Hunter, one day I'll tell you about my lack of love for mashed potatoes." She smirked.

"Fine. Another time, but now," he slid back over on top of her and claimed her mouth.

He didn't have to finish the sentence. She knew exactly what was on his mind.

And she loved it.

Epilogue

DEREK HOLLISTER SAT at one of his new discoveries, a nice upscale bar several blocks from city center. He'd lived in Houston for twelve years and being single he ate out a lot. How he'd never heard of Bogart's, he didn't know. But he dug it.

He needed to unwind. That night, Thursday, he sat back at a corner table, lounging on the leather banquette, and sipping a single malt.

Tomorrow, he'd hit the gym and work out his stress. His frickin' CEO and his big damn mouth.

No, we're not gonna see numbers skyrocket next quarter. This is not just a bump in the road, he sarcastically told himself as if having a conversation with the man right then.

He sighed and took another sip, hoping the liquor would drown the memories of the investor call.

A livelier group gathered at the far end of the bar,

apparently celebrating something. It appeared to be mostly couples but also a few single men and women stood and chatted. Derek caught a glimpse of wrapped presents and gift bags on a side table. Yup, looked to be an engagement party.

Good for them.

Marriage wasn't for him, but it was good for some.

The bride-to-be stood in the center of the group, wearing a broad white smile and sporting a nice rock. A brunet man held her hand, occasionally kissing it and whispering in her ear. He must be the smitten groom.

Whoa! Hold up.

A woman leaned in and handed the bride a fresh drink. They clinked glasses. Who the hell was she? She didn't appear to have a man in tow.

He scanned her from top to bottom—brown hair with highlights, expensive-looking top and fitted skirt, high heels to show off her gorgeous gams. She was probably five-nine, but in those heels... damn. At six-three, he appreciated a taller woman.

Damn!

He couldn't peel his eyes away. Still no apparent boyfriend in sight.

She carried herself like a confident woman. She likely had a job where she was in charge, and if not, she probably should be in charge.

He watched her for several minutes.

Intriguing creature. He could read her body language

like a map—warm and friendly with some, reserved and posed with others.

He *had* to learn more about this woman.

She walked to the end of the bar top and smiled at the bartender as she spoke.

Fuck! Her painted red lips were staggering.

"Lexi," he heard the bride call, "get one for Hunter."

The woman nodded, then smoothed her hair behind her left ear.

Oh yeah! No ring. He would definitely need to find out more about *Lexi*. The sooner the better.

Thank you!

Please look for Lexi's story, Only Chance at Love, at your favorite book retailers.

If you enjoyed this story, please consider posting a review at one or more of your favorite book retailers. Even a short review, one or two lines, can be a tremendous encouragement to the author. Your review is also a gift to other readers who may be searching for just this sort of story and will be grateful that you helped them find it.

Thank you!

Other Books by Mia London

Honeymoon Hideaway

Runaway (Cascade Mountain Manhunt, 1)
Renegade (Cascade Mountain Manhunt, 2)

Accidental Tryst

Life To The Max
Wanton Angel, Prequel to Life To The Max

Perfect Seduction (Perfect, 1)
Perfect Surrender (Perfect, 2)

Beyond Lace (Hard Men of the Rockies, 4)

Undeniable Fate (Undeniable, 1)
Undeniable Love (Undeniable, 2)

Dry Spell (Sweet Escape, 1)
Hot Spell (Sweet Escape, 2)
Cold Spell (Sweet Escape, 3)

About the Author

Mia London loves to write.
After reading fiction for years, she decided it was finally
time to put those images and scenes floating around in her
head down on paper.

She is a huge fan of romance, highly optimistic, and wildly faithful to the HEA (happily ever after). Her goal is to create a fantasy you will enjoy with characters you could love.

She lives in Texas with her attentive, loving, super-model husband, and perfectly behaved, brilliant children. Her produce never wilts, there are no weeds in her flowerbeds and chocolate is her favorite food group.

Facebook

Twitter

Instagram

Goodreads

www.mialondon.com

Email: mia@mialondon.com